Sky Dancer

Other Romance Books by Kathleen Wells

Unconditional Love
New Heights
Midnight Gold

SKY DANCER

Kathleen Wells
Treble Heart Books

SKY DANCER
Copyright © 2001
By Kathleen Wells
All rights reserved.

Cover design:
Copyright 2000 © Lee Emory
All rights reserved.

Treble Heart Books
1284 Overlook Dr.
Sierra Vista, AZ 85635-5512

http://www.trebleheartbooks.com

ISBN: 1-931742-30-8

Dedication

This story is dedicated to our daughter and her family: Kim, Peter, Lacey, and Jeffrey. Thank you for always being there for me. May you all find that special love in your lives and learn to dance with the angels.

CHAPTER ONE

This morning's hearing had been as successful as the maiden voyage of the Titanic. It accomplished nothing, and AJ MacKenzie's hopes for a speedy trial sank with the hollow smack of a gavel. She was no closer to seeing the indictment of the man who swindled her father and neighbors than she had been months ago when his deception became clear. Slime like William Jorgensen always oozed through the cracks of justice.

Disgust rippled through her body. She'd been raised to believe in American justice and the theory that bad guys did big time for their transgressions. Now she wasn't so sure.

AJ climbed on to the pontoon of her amphibious DeHavilland Beaver and threw her bags in the baggage compartment. She jumped to the tarmac and moved toward her restored '57 Corvette. A crisp, early fall breeze blew across her cheeks. Hair whipped around her face, and she tucked loose waves behind her ear.

She smiled as some of her impotent frustration faded. Power and freedom. That's what she felt when she drove her 'vette. The only thing better than racing the car was flying, dancing among the clouds. She couldn't wait to take off for the northern reaches of Canada. This day was about to get better. A flight always made things right.

Grabbing another load of gear she climbed up on the plane. The logo, "Sky Dancer Aeronautics, Roy MacKenzie and Daughter," never failed to bring a smile to her lips.

AJ jumped down and went for the final load.

She gathered up the purchases from a hurried shopping excursion, silently cursing the slippery plastic bags. *No time to pack. They'll have to go like this.*

Loop handles cut into her fingers as the heavy bags twisted together and slid from her hands. Packages scattered on the ground.

"Damn!" AJ stooped to gather them into a small pile. She collided with a man who'd bent to help her. "Thanks." She raised her brow and offered the stranger her hand. "Mister...?"

"Satterfield," he answered, grasping her fingers warmly. "Dan Satterfield."

Well, some people still know how to treat others. Her gaze slid over the man's body. Sheer animal attraction kicked her in the stomach, before she forced her attention to the belongings she'd scattered on the pavement.

They gathered the packages and slowly rose to face each other.

"Thanks again for your help. I hate these darn bags." AJ shook her head. "Was there something you needed?"

"I'm here for my flight."

Recognition hit her. "Oh, I'm sorry. You're my passenger. The name didn't connect. Dad told me about you."

"You haven't told me who *you* are. Pilot? Secretary? Sidekick?" His voice was low, seductive and teasing.

She looked him over slowly. Brand new outdoor clothing with the distinctive style of L.L. Bean covered his tight athletic body. He could have just stepped off one of their catalogue pages.

A cocky smile curved his lips, as if he knew he had been assessed. Sunlight danced off his chestnut hair, highlighting reddish gold tints among thick waves. The sheer charisma of the man made her heart pop into her throat. Heat rose in her cheeks as a delicate flush undoubtedly crept onto her face.

She swallowed around a lump of anticipation. "AJ—AJ MacKenzie. I'll be flying you north."

A boyish grin spread across his face. "I've never been flown by a woman." Laugh lines crinkled the corners of his eyes, making them smile as much as his lips.

He looked into her eyes, his face a fraction of an inch from hers. Warm breath fluttered across her face. Wintergreen tickled her nose.

She saw promise flash across his face. But a promise of what?

"Who are you?"

"I told you, Dan...."

"No. You're dressed like an outdoorsman." Her gaze traveled up and down the length of him. "At least a new, store-bought version of one." AJ grasped Dan's hand, palm up. "Your hands are the hands of an impostor. Soft—and straight from a boardroom or a bank."

Even as she said it, AJ knew her dad would be appalled by her confrontation of this passenger.

"What difference does that make?" He sounded defensive.

"I suppose it doesn't."

But it did. Daniel Satterfield was an intriguing enigma. She wanted to find out what made him tick, and hoped she wouldn't find a reason to distrust him. After months of dealing with a slick con man like Jorgensen, AJ had grown skeptical of anyone who wasn't what he appeared to be.

"It's simple. I work and live in Chicago. I like to fish for big ones that put up a good fight." He shrugged. "They're in Canada. You want the job or not?"

Business, this guy is just business! They needed every customer to keep Sky Dancer flying.

"Certainly." She gave him a cocky little bow. "Sky Dancer Aeronautics, at your service." AJ turned away and walked to his pile of gear. "Help me, and we'll load up and take off."

"Right," Dan said as he moved to her side, muttering. "I can't wait."

"It's pretty late in the year, Mr. Satterfield..."

"Dan."

"Dan," she repeated. "What if the weather turns bad, and I can't get to where you're camped? I'd need to meet at an alternative pickup point. Can you do that?"

"No problem. I've done wilderness hiking. I have everything I need to hold out for a few extra days if I have to." He flashed a quirky grin. "Not counting all the fish I'm going to catch. I'll get the rest of my equipment."

She couldn't help it. AJ wondered what kind of equipment her client had. The shape of his body suggested lean, hard muscles. Strength and endurance. *He's a client.*

With his camping and fishing gear loaded, they climbed into the plane. AJ ignored the throbbing of her heart as she settled into the pilot seat. She'd never flown such an attractive client. Certainly never one she'd had a physical interest in. Lust, she chided herself. Sheer, unadulterated lust. Get your hormones back on business.

AJ looked at him and smiled. Dan Satterfield was going to have the ride of his life. She'd make sure of that. Drawing her gaze away from him, she snapped her harness across her chest.

When she fastened her harness, Dan did the same, then watched her start her safety check.

What a catch. I'd love to net this one. Thinking about her had his palms sweating and his heart speeding up. He pictured her body, boyishly slim with subtle curves, but a perfectly heart shaped rear. And those eyes—as blue as a Jamaican bay. Fresh and young, she seemed innocent, yet there was a wildness to her he'd love to explore. A sigh slipped from his lips. *Damn. She's got me thinking like a teenager.* He shook his head in disgust.

He'd never seen anything quite like that hair. So iridescent black, it reflected all the colors of the rainbow. A scrap of blue-green fabric secured her hair at the nape of her neck. He'd love to untie that scarf and run his fingers through the long waves.

She was a bush pilot that looked like sweet sin. Yep, he'd definitely like to know her better. What would a relationship with her be like? It sure wouldn't be dull. He'd bet on that.

I'd love to get her in the woods for a few days.

His thoughts stopped abruptly as the engine revved and the plane raced down the runway, lifting into the air without the slightest bump.

He let his breath escape in a relieved whoosh and she looked at him with open curiosity.

"You *have* flown in a small plane, haven't you? I thought you'd chartered in here before."

"A few times."

His hands were clenched in white-knuckled fists in his lap, and he fought to loosen them. As he flexed his fingers to get the blood moving again, he watched every move AJ made. Impressed with her competence, he gradually relaxed.

She banked the plane, dropping the wing on his side of the cabin. Dan felt suspended from heaven with only a thread to stop his fall to earth. Fear gripped his insides, dampness covered his forehead. Free fall ending in death seemed imminent. He survived the turn as he suspected one does roller coaster loops and dips. Only he'd been smart enough to stay off of carnival rides. Dan fought his traitorous stomach as she leveled the plane.

They passed the tip of Lake Nipigon, and quickly left behind the small towns of Southern Canada as well as the few roads and railroads in the area.

"What's the road down there cutting through the trees?"

"Trans Canada Highway. It's the last big one we'll cross."

Dan's attention wavered from AJ's voice. He watched the way her graceful, competent hands caressed the yoke. She seemed to cherish this plane as though it was a living being.

AJ cleared her throat. "I said, have you flown into this area before?"

"What do your initials stand for?"

"What?"

"Your initials—what's your name?"

She grimaced. "That's not really important. Have you...?"

"It's not important, but I'm curious about why an attractive woman uses initials instead of her name."

Dan watched her face. Embarrassment fought with irritation. Hesitancy fluttered there. He thought she wasn't going to answer. "What is it? Some old fashioned thing?"

Still she hesitated.

"Let me guess. Agatha—Augusta—Abigail?"

"All right, already." She laughed, then answered quietly, "Aurora Jean."

"Aurora Jean." He wrapped his tongue around it. "That's beautiful. Why on earth don't you use it?"

"I was a tomboy. I didn't like having such a feminine tag. My father named me for the aurora borealis that was showing the night I was born. The Jean is for my mother." AJ pushed a loose bit of hair away from her face. "So," she asked again, "have you flown in here before?"

"Just once with a friend."

"I thought you said you'd been up a few times."

"Well, here only once. In a small company jet several times."

She gave an unladylike snort. "A company jet hardly equates with flying in a prop job."

"They're both too small for my liking," Dan said. "My friend's a commercial pilot. We came here to hunt and fish, but he couldn't get away this time." He shrugged. "I decided to go it alone."

"What do you do?" she asked.

"I design computer software." Dan hesitated, his voice somber. "I didn't want to go into the business, but Dad needed me." He wanted to smack his forehead with his fist. *Why on earth did I tell her that?*

AJ lifted one brow. "You don't sound enthused."

"It's okay."

A frown flitted across his face before he hid it behind a mask of indifference. He changed the subject.

"What's that little town down there?"

"That's Nakina, the last settlement we'll fly directly over. There's one more between here and the lake, but we'll miss it."

When she absently tucked a loose strand of hair behind her ear, he noticed a tiny silver biplane swinging from her earlobe.

"Are you fishing for northern pike?" she asked.

He looked at her delicate profile and swallowed hard. "Yeah. I want to catch northerns. That's right."

He fought to focus on the words instead of the woman. Dan pulled a packet of thick, pink wintergreen candies from his pocket and extended the bag to AJ. With a smile, she took one and slipped it between her lips licking the sweet dust from her fingertips slowly, unthinkingly sensuous. Dan nearly swallowed his tongue. Could he get her to go with him, he wondered. His gut told him he'd be missing something very special if he let this woman slip through his fingers.

"AJ, what are you going to do while I fish for ten days? Are you going home?"

"Nope. I'm going on to Lake Opinnagua to do some camping and fishing. I'm looking forward to some time off by myself." She shifted the candy to the other side of her mouth, licking her lips in the process, obviously savoring the flavor.

Dan watched, unable to stop a groan as he imagined those lips on his. The silence between them grew and Dan tried to get control of his emotions as a tightness grew in his pants.

"What's on your mind, Dan?"

Startled, he refocused. "I was thinking about solitary vacations. Gets lonely. You could stay at the lake where I'll be." He plunged ahead, as confused as a teenager. "In your own camp, of course. We could get to know each other. If you're interested that is." He sent her a questioning look.

Her gaze met his. His stomach bucked like a plane in turbulence. He hadn't felt that kind of kick from a woman in a long time.

"I don't know," AJ said.

He opened his mouth to encourage her. A mouth suddenly as dry and crackly as last year's pine needles. His thoughts failed him. "Why?"

"I don't think that's a good idea. I need time alone and you probably do, too. We'll just go as planned."

"It could be interesting. Sitting around a campfire, telling stories. Keeping each other company. Reconsider, Aurora?"

His voice wrapped sensuously around her name like an early morning mist hugging the ferns.

AJ appeared to concentrate on her flying. Her voice stayed level. "Not this time." She shook her head and sent him a regret-filled smile.

He heard her regret and saw the slight slump of her shoulders that accompanied it. She wanted to say yes, but couldn't.

"You're afraid of me, aren't you?" he asked.

"No! Well—maybe a little. But that doesn't matter. It's just not a good idea."

Disappointment slammed into Dan. "Are you sure?"

AJ shook her head. "Sorry. I don't date clients."

"Fair enough. I don't have to like it, but that's always a wise choice."

"Hold on." She aimed the DeHavilland toward earth, and Dan's stomach catapulted into his throat. By the time she pulled out of the short dive, his pulse vibrated like a jackhammer.

They approached a narrow ribbon of water that split the thick forest. An expanse of reeds and water lilies stretched on both sides of the creek before giving way to Douglas fir and lodge pole pine.

"Look down there," AJ said.

He spotted moose at the water's edge. A cow and her weanling calf stood knee deep in water, pulling at the long grasses that grew between the floating pads. The sound of AJ's plane caused their ears to flick forward as they looked up. Apparently not frightened by what they saw or heard, they resumed their peaceful grazing.

"Beautiful, aren't they?"

Dan laughed at her description. "I've heard them called a lot of things, but beautiful isn't one of them. They are intriguing creatures, though." He turned his gaze to her beaming face. "You really love it up here, don't you?"

"Yes, I do. I've spent lots of time here, and my ancestors were in Canada for generations before most of them moved south into the states. Most of the Native American side stayed north and the Scots went south."

"You handle this plane like you were born in it."

"Might as well have been. I was raised in it. Both my grandfather and father were bush pilots. They taught me how to fly before I could ride a bike." She smiled. "What about you? Ever had the urge to take the controls?"

"I don't know. Never thought about it." He looked quickly away from her.

"Dan!"

He turned and saw her "aha" expression.

"You're afraid to, aren't you?" she asked.

"No. I just never had time," Dan answered indignantly. He dodged any further questions. "What about your mother? Does she fly?"

Silence settled, thick and heavy in the cabin for a split second.

"My mother's dead." The shake of her head stopped his apology, then her attention drifted back to the controls.

Dan cleared his throat. "So, tell me—Sky Dancer's pretty obvious with that upside down plane on your hat. You really do that stuff?"

"Sure! Want me to show you?" AJ tipped a wing and revved the engine.

"Hell no! I don't mind flying," *much* he thought, "but I'll take mine upright, thank you very much."

Her laugh filled the cabin. "Someday maybe you'll trust me enough to let me show you what it's like."

"Did your dad teach you?"

"Not hardly." She chuckled. "He didn't want me doing stunts at all. A friend taught me."

"So your dad objected, huh?"

"That's an understatement, and Charlie, he's our mechanic, ratted on me all the time. I came in one day, and Charlie was waiting on the dock. He'd seen me doing loops and rolls and was fit to be tied." She shook her head with a smile. "Told me he'd tell Pop and see to it I got grounded if I didn't promise to stop."

"But you didn't."

"I could give up breathing easier than flying. So, I stood there on the dock, hung my head, and swore I'd quit." She chuckled again. "I had my fingers crossed behind my back, of course. From then on, I made sure I did my aerobatics well away from the house and hangar so they wouldn't see me."

"So what's so special about it?"

"Hmm, I never really thought about it. I guess it's being up here alone, the quiet hum of the engine, the rush of air past the cockpit, looping and dancing in the clouds. It's positively spiritual. There's nothing better."

"Nothing?"

AJ's cheeks turned a delightful pink. "Well, almost nothing," she said glancing at her watch and peering off to her left.

Dan noticed her frown and spoke up. "Problem?"

"No. At least I don't think so, but we should have seen Ogoki by now." She looked at her compass and then checked her map. "Maybe we're slightly off course." Tucking the map down beside her seat, she tapped her finger against the glass of the compass.

"Could we have passed it while we were talking?"

"No. I was watching for landmarks."

"You make it sound like you're navigating around the neighborhood."

"I am. I know this forest as well as my own yard. At least from up here. If I showed you how, you'd pick it up right away. Besides, you design computer programs and you think navigation sounds difficult. You gotta' be kidding!"

"I guess it all depends on your natural talents."

"Speaking of which, I'll bet your natural talent is management. You know, control."

"Control?" Dan shifted uncomfortably.

"Yeah, like being in the driver's seat. I'll bet at your company you like to know everything that goes on."

He thought of the endless board, production and marketing meetings he hustled to each day, hurrying from place to place, grabbing a cold sandwich and colder coffee on the run. All the tasks he could delegate to his lead people but refused to relinquish.

"Bull's-eye. Guilty as charged."

"I think you'd be much more comfortable if you were flying this plane."

Dan felt the blood drain from his face. "I'm no pilot."

"It's as easy as driving a car, honestly. And I have dual

controls. If you have any trouble, I'll take it back in a split second."

Dan thought of his best friend in college. The one who ended up splattered on a runway during a flying lesson. "No thanks. I'm fine with you flying this bird."

"You'd be amazed at the difference it makes to have the controls, just like in a car. Give it a try."

"No way."

"Oh, come on. It's easy."

"No."

"Dan, it's really not difficult."

"I control what I'm familiar with. I'm smart enough to know what I *don't* know."

"You aren't afraid, are you? Come on. I dare ya."

He shook his head.

AJ grinned. "Double dare ya."

Dan remembered boyhood taunts, dares to do the kind of things that broke boys arms when the dare went wrong, and groaned. "You'll be sorry you said that. I never pass up a double dare. Couldn't when I was a kid and still don't."

With a skeptical look, Dan gingerly grasped the yoke with both hands. AJ let go and the plane dipped. Dan's jaw clamped as he concentrated and, with her guidance, brought the plane level while he managed to keep it steady.

"Hey—this isn't so bad." Pleased with himself, a smile spread across Dan's face.

"Told you it would make a difference. You don't even think about being worried when you have control, do you?"

"Not at all. This is great," he exclaimed.

He was in control. Invincible. Nothing could happen.

Wrong!

The engine died.

Silence engulfed the cabin.

"Damn! What happened? AJ, what the hell happened?"

"You broke my plane," she yelled, grabbing the yoke and jerking the headset on at the same time.

"What's happening?" he demanded.

His stomach took a nose dive as she flipped switches. The only answer was useless clicks. The engine wouldn't restart.

Wanting desperately for this to be some kind of joke, Dan looked sideways at her. "Look, if you're trying to show off, this is going too far. I don't find this a bit funny. Fire this thing up again."

"I don't play practical jokes, Satterfield." She checked her fuel gage.

AJ flipped on the radio. "Mayday, mayday. This is DeHavilland two-two-zero-four-Victor. We are east-northeast of Nakina. Engine failure. Making a forced landing. Anybody read me? Mayday, mayday."

Dan heard no response. AJ tried twice more, then yanked off the headset and threw it down.

"That's dead. We're going in. Fold your jacket," AJ ordered. "Tighten those shoulder straps. When we come down, put your jacket in front of your face to protect your head."

For a split second, Dan and AJ looked at each other. Nothing in her expression suggested she couldn't handle this situation. Fear forced a lump large enough to choke a moose into his throat. He did as she instructed with unsteady hands.

The plane glided down on silent wings. Dan scanned the forest for a break in the trees. Losing altitude rapidly, he feared AJ would have only one chance to put the plane down safely, then she turned the plane toward a tiny break in the canopy.

"You're not putting it down there are you?" Dan demanded.

AJ nodded and stared at the rapidly approaching ground. He saw sunlight glance off a body of water barely large enough to be a pond and watched as she dropped toward the water. The pontoons hit the glassy surface. The plane bounced once then raced across the lake.

"Damn thing's too small!" Dan shouted.

"Brace yourself. We're going to hit!" AJ yelled. She gripped the yoke as it jerked and pulled, bucking in her hands.

Dan braced against the control panel a moment before they passed the end of the lake and catapulted onto dry land. Metal screamed as the pontoons ripped from the fuselage of the DeHavilland. Sliding on its belly, the plane slammed nose first into the pine forest.

A terrible screeching echoed through the forest.

Gargantuan trees ripped off the wings and grabbed at the skin of the plane. Limbs crashed around them as it slowed. An enveloping cloud of dirt, flying bark and dried pine needles mushroomed up.

Dan lifted his head and heard AJ's forehead hit the yoke with a resounding crack. They bounced off a giant pine, and she snapped against the harness.

His head rapped the side window as the fuselage caved in and captured his legs. Twisted metal slammed to a stop. He lifted a hand toward AJ before dizziness overcame him.

Moments later he slid into a black bottomless hole.

CHAPTER TWO

AJ moaned as she broke through the fog numbing her brain. A thick cloud of dirt and crushed needles rose through the trees like a giant fern pushing toward the light. A tiny spiral of smoke drifted beside the crushed hull of her plane. Dried pine snapped and crackled as fire sprang to life. The burning smell assaulted her senses, and she jerked awake.

"Dan," she yelled, terrified. Silence. "Dan?"

Nothing!

Her client lay slumped against his harness, motionless, his face the color of paste.

"Come on, Dan, answer me." Fear rippled through her. They didn't have time to hang around. They had to get out of there. She laid a trembling hand on his chest. He was breathing—barely.

Her relief was short-lived. Smoke curled upward to her shattered window. A shiver of terror quaked through her body.

"We've got to get out of here. Damn it—snap out of it! We have to go."

No response.

Panic gripped her nerves and stole her breath. Dan's side of the crushed fuselage pressed against his right leg. He was trapped.

She popped open his belts and tried to pull him toward her. His lower body wouldn't budge.

"Damn, double damn! Okay, okay," she muttered. "Keep it together girl or neither of you will get out of this."

She pulled her lower lip between her teeth and concentrated as she laid Dan against the seat and looked for something to pry him from the wreckage. A memory leapt across her mind. One of a young mother, her legs trapped in the crushed hull of another plane. AJ's breath rattled out. *I won't lose another person like this.*

Frantically she swung her gaze from side to side. Finding nothing useful, she turned and braced her back against the cabin wall and swung her legs across Dan's body. Using both feet, she pushed as hard as she could against the steel trap. It held. Temper and fear flared at once. Again she pushed and again the metal refused to move.

Flames licked at the sides of the plane. Terror threatened to consume her as effectively as the growing heat. Sweat soaked her body plastering cloth to skin.

She kicked out with the heel of her boot. "Sonofabitch!" Burning tears of frustration welled in her eyes and a lump swelled in her throat. Scooting down into her seat to get better leverage, she braced against the twisted metal.

The black smoke invading the cabin choked her. Blind panic pumped adrenaline into her blood and gave her added strength. "One, two, three, shove." The door moved a fraction.

Again! She held her breath and shoved with all her might. The hull gave way with a reluctant groan. It was enough. Sweat burned her eyes, so she wiped her arm across them while she fought for air in the dense smoke.

This time when she pulled, Dan fell against her chest. Chestnut hair brushed against her cheek. A package of pink wintergreen lozenges slipped from his pocket. It was silly, but she smiled and crammed them back into his jacket.

She opened the door and backed out, kicking bits of burning debris aside. Grasping Dan under his arms, she dragged his dead weight backward. As his legs cleared the seat, she lost her balance and fell sideways.

In the dirt and pine duff, with Dan sprawled across her body, she tried to catch her breath. The flames leaped higher and spread. She had no time to waste. She jumped up and pulled him away from the fire.

AJ left him in the dirt, jerked a bandanna from her hip pocket and tied it over her face as she ran back to the plane. It was beyond help, but they needed their survival gear.

Grabbing the extinguisher behind her seat, she sprayed foam on the plane and ground around it. The lather quickly reduced tree branches and pine needles to a smoldering pile.

The empty canister hung limply in her hand. She threw it to the ground with a sob, and slipped the bandanna off her face as her eyes loosed a flood of tears. They ran unchecked down her face. Her father's plane, the plane she'd grown up in, was gone.

Despair threatened to crush her. She drew a deep, jagged breath and squared her sagging shoulders. Dan needed her. With determination in her stride, AJ went to check on him.

She knelt behind his unconscious form. Moisture oozed down her face and mingled with dried tears as she lifted his upper body and stretched her arms around his broad chest. A scarlet drop hit the back of her hand, then another. She stopped tugging against his weight and gently lifted her fingertips to her face. A gash lanced across her forehead. Her fingers came away sticky with blood. Pain pulsed around the wound. A quick swipe of her sleeve cleared some of the mess from her eyes. Ignoring her pain, she locked her hands over Dan's chest to drag him to a moss carpet under the trees.

Slumping beside him to catch her breath, she turned her attention to her injured client. Gently, she shook his shoulder.

"Dan. Wake up. Can you hear me?"

No answer.

She ran her hands over his solid body in search of injuries. He had a body AJ assumed had been honed in the company gym. Ripples of firm muscle lay hidden beneath his flannel shirt and pants. Soft warmth started in the center of her body and spread like wildfire. The urge to touch his skin hit her with such force she sat back on her heels and simply stared at his unconscious figure. His expression reflected gentleness, even innocence, she wouldn't expect from a business executive.

Great! We're stuck in the middle of nowhere and your hormones are salsa dancing with your brain.

She shook her head and pain shot through it. Again she focused on Dan. Other than a bump on his head, she couldn't find anything major. Nothing appeared to be broken or badly damaged. She prayed there were no internal injuries. If the plane's locator was knocked out and they had to stay put, they'd have a long wait for a rescue party.

AJ's emotions swam in a churning stream—fear, rage, longing. She couldn't sort them out. Minutes passed while she waited and fought for control. When the smoke dissipated, she pulled supplies from the wreckage. Dan moaned and she hurried to his side. Relieved to see him coming around, AJ dropped to her knees beside him.

"Dan?" AJ brushed her hair out of her face, impatient with the tumbled mass. "How you doin'?"

He rolled his head toward her as though it was too heavy to lift. She watched as he tried to focus on her face. "AJ, what happened? Your face! Are you all right?" He lifted a shaky hand to her forehead and tried to sit up. He grimaced then groaned. She eased him down and waited for his pain to subside.

"What is it? Where do you hurt?"

"It's my leg."

"Is it broken?"

"No. Old injury." A low rumble came from his throat. AJ cringed and wished she could ease his pain; instead she could only hope to lighten the tension. "You're too young for Vietnam. College jock? Football?"

"Sort of." Dan looked sheepish. "Slipped in the showers."

She choked back a chuckle as his face tightened.

"It's dislocated," he slurred. "What about your head?"

"I'm okay. I'll take care of it in a minute. Let's check you out."

He tried to sit up again and she frowned. "Are you sure you should move before we fix this?"

"Yeah. I'm okay."

Slowly, she helped him move back to rest against a tree. Each movement he made wrenched a low growl from his lips.

She frowned at the pain reflected on his face. "Do you know how to fix it? I got our stuff out including a medical kit."

"Yeah. I can fix it. How'd you get me out?"

"Adrenaline I guess. The plane started to burn." Her eyes filled with tears as she forced herself to ignore her misery. "That's not important." She jumped up before he could ask more questions and went to get the first aid supplies.

"Which knee is it?" she asked, sinking down beside him.

"Right." He grunted. Perspiration dripped from his forehead, crossing his pale gray skin. Beads of sweat gathered on his upper lip and a tiny muscle twitched in his jaw.

"I've got to cut these pretty, brand new pants of yours, so I can get to it." She grinned at him.

"So I like new clothes on vacation. Big deal," he grumbled back at her. She noted the crooked little grin on his lips.

"All right then. Let's get this done. We'll get you into some warmer clothes before nightfall."

At his silent nod, she pulled a pair of bandage scissors from the kit and cut back the material to reveal a rapidly swelling leg. Sweat rolled down his cheeks and dripped onto the collar of his shirt. AJ pulled a couple of pain pills from the kit and handed him a canteen of water and the medicine. He shook his head, refusing them.

"Come on, Dan." She frowned as he clenched his jaw against obvious pain. "There's no need to be in so much discomfort."

"I'm okay," he grunted.

"For Pete's sake, stop being macho. This is going to hurt like a son-of-a-gun. Now take these and let me get to work. We have to do this after they take effect and then think about what we're going to do to get out of here. It's a long way to a settlement."

Reluctantly he took the pills. Thirty minutes later, he directed her as she put his knee back in place and applied two splints and elastic wraps to keep it immobile. As she finished tying off the bandages, he sank back against the tree.

With a towel from the kit, she wiped the sweat and dirt from his face then sat back on her heels to look at him. He drifted into a state of semi-consciousness once more. She let her fingertips glide across his forehead and down the length of his strong jaw. The thought of losing this virtual stranger brought a tightness to her throat she failed to understand. She knew intuitively that it was more than not wanting to be responsible for his death. She had known him literally hours and felt a closer bond to him than anyone she had ever known.

Long sienna lashes rimmed his closed eyes. The pain appeared dulled, his mouth was no longer tense, his lips relaxed in a near smile. Regret trembled through her. She'd gotten him into this, goaded him into taking the controls and then this happened. He'd never trust her now.

"I'm sorry," she whispered. "I'll get you home, Dan. I promise." Quietly she stood up and left him resting while she finished unloading their equipment.

Tying her hair out of the way, she cleaned her face and bandaged the gash on her forehead. Tenderness spread from under the gauze, and she hurt all over. The muscles in her back were taut, burning. Beyond that, she was all right physically. Her heart was another matter. The loss of her father's old plane was devastating. She shook her head as angry tears threatened to overflow.

Get over it. The plane was just a machine, not flesh and blood. Be glad you're alive.

Determined to get a grip on her emotions, she built a fire and started supper moving around the stone ring, working over the flames with practiced ease. There was a slight chill in the early evening air, so AJ covered Dan with a blanket as he slept.

Busy at the fire, she didn't realize she was being watched until the hair at the base of her neck bristled. AJ swung part way around. "Well, you're back. How do you feel?"

"Better, thanks. Considering..."

His tone grated on already raw nerves. She stopped what she was doing and straightened from the fire. "Considering what?"

"Considering I survived your plane crash."

Disappointment in his tone hit her first, followed quickly by a flash of temper. "*My* plane crash. You think this was my fault?"

"These things don't just happen do they? When was that plane overhauled last?"

"For your information, Charlie and I went over her yesterday. That plane was in perfect condition."

"Obviously not or this wouldn't have happened. Engines don't just die."

AJ fought to hold onto her temper. Maybe his pain was making him grouchy. The whole thing had her ready to rip his face off, or anything else that got too close. She took a calming breath and answered. "I did a last minute check of everything, made sure there weren't any broken bolts or anything. Anyway, I resent your implication."

"I'm not implying anything. I'm just trying to understand what happened."

"Well understand this, if it hadn't been me flying that plane you would have kissed your butt good-bye. Not every pilot could have landed in a place like this and walked away from it."

"In my business you have to be practical and analytical. I believe everything happens for a reason, and, in my experience, it's usually carelessness."

Her temper erupted into a ball of flame. "I saved your sorry butt! Maybe I should have left you in the plane and let it burn!"

Upset by the destruction of her plane, she was angry and hurt that he thought this had been her fault. The lack of his support and approval cut deeper than she expected. Only one man's opinion ever mattered to her before, her father's. Now his plane was gone. Her eyes wet, AJ spun back to the fire and violently stirred to mush the canned stew bubbling in the pot.

Dan sighed. "Do you have any idea what happened?"

"It's a little late to ask since you think I crashed it deliberately."

"I'm sorry, AJ. I guess I'm more shaken up by this than I realized."

She looked at him thoughtfully. "I'm sorry about the crash and about you being hurt." Her chest constricted as a giant fist gripped her heart. "I'm really sorry to lose this plane. I assure you the Beaver was in top notch condition." She sucked in a deep breath. "I don't have a death wish. Up here you better have a good plane, or you could be in big trouble."

"So," Dan asked quietly, "what *do* you think happened?"

The image of her Nemesis, Jorgensen, in a five-hundred-dollar suit, flashing rings and slicked back hair popped into her mind's eye. The con man would do anything to reach his own goals, stepping over anyone who got in his way. She shivered at the thought of being close to him in any way.

AJ shook her head to clear the ugly picture. "I'd like to say I haven't a clue, but I'm afraid I do."

"What are you talking about?"

A heavy sigh slid from her chest. "Nothing. I don't want to go into until I know for sure. In the morning, I'll see if I can tell what the problem was. Maybe I can get the radio working."

"Doesn't the plane have one of those automatic locator things?"

"Yeah, and my bet is, it isn't working."

"What makes you think so?"

She looked him straight in the eyes. "I didn't crash this plane, Dan. I think somebody set us up. Whoever did this was smart enough to knock out the transponder, too."

"You mean sabotage?"

"I'm afraid so. I'll find out tomorrow. Now, how 'bout some dinner?"

He hesitated as though ready to argue, then said, "Sounds great, thanks. I didn't realize how hungry I was. I must have been asleep for hours."

"Four, if anybody's counting."

"Did you get some rest, too?"

"I've been busy getting our stuff together and figuring out what we'll need to take with us if the radio won't work."

He looked confused as she handed him a plate of stew and a cup of coffee. "Take? Where are we going?"

She sat down with her food. "If we can't raise anyone on the radio, we have to get out of here before an early winter has a chance to set in. With your leg, it will take us two or three weeks of walking. That's not even counting if we have to hole up for bad weather. We have to move before it's too late."

"I thought you were supposed to stay put."

"You are, but in this case we can't afford to. This forest is too dense. They don't know where we went down and, in fact, they won't even miss us for ten days." She sighed thoughtfully.

"No one at the airport expects to hear from us. Dad probably won't, because I told him I'd talk to him in a couple weeks. He doesn't expect a message from me until I get you back. We're on our own, Dan." She added quietly, "No one's looking for us."

They finished eating their stew in silence, and then AJ took the plates down to the lake to rinse them thinking of what lay ahead.

Dusk descended while she was at the lake and the dancing flames of the campfire guided her back to Dan. The wood she added to the fire created yellow and red arms that stretched toward the darkened sky. Occasionally the wood dropped further into the consuming blaze sending sparks drifting skyward. Around the camp, shadows cast by the light shivered as a chilly breeze swayed the trees around their clearing.

AJ slipped the plates into her backpack and turned to Dan. "You get some sleep. We're a long way from home, and I need you walking tomorrow. Think you'll manage?"

"Sure, but I've been thinking," Dan said. "Here's what we're going to do."

AJ frowned at him. "I beg your pardon?"

"I have a plan. We'll spend a week here letting my leg heal. If no one comes looking, we'll head due south as fast as possible. Then..."

"Wait just a darn minute." She stood, hands on hips, her shoulders rigid.

"I'm the pilot of this plane and that puts me in charge. No, wait." She held up her hand to stop his protest. "I'm not finished. I know this forest and you don't, and I know what we have to do to get out of this alive."

"We have plenty of supplies. I say we should wait."

"Dan, you have to rely on me—to trust me."

She watched as he looked her over as though assessing what he saw. AJ knew he was used to giving orders, of being in charge.

He wouldn't be one to readily accept direction from others, especially from a woman.

He hesitated. "All right, Aurora, but if I don't agree with what you're doing I'm going to say so."

"Fine. We can't risk winter coming in and catching us. We head out tomorrow. I know it's early, but let's get some sleep. It's going to be a tough trip."

She turned abruptly and moved to her own sleeping bag. "Good night, Dan." Her body crushed the dried pine needles she had piled into make-shift mattresses releasing a fresh burst of scent.

In the encompassing darkness, she looked across the flames of the dying fire and watched the light shimmer off the feathered highlights of Dan's hair. His eyes had closed instantly, deep even breathing indicating he was already asleep.

He looked boyish like this, but she was sure he would be a man-eating grizzly in the business world. What was a CEO type like him doing out in the middle of a forest fishing? Shouldn't he be on a beach on the French Riviera with a beautiful blonde at his side?

A small sigh escaped her lips. She'd never be a fair skinned beauty more comfortable in high fashion than boots. Sadness threatened but she pushed it aside. *What difference does it make? He can have all the raving beauties he wants.* She looked at the colors of the fire, listened to the sounds of the forest. *I have all I want right here.*

Aggravated with herself for even thinking of things that would never be part of her, she shook her head, rolled onto her back and looked at the night sky. Beneath her, the needles crackled and bunched up as she shifted her weight to burrow down and make a comfortable bed from the lumpy heap. This was where she belonged, where she wanted to be. Looking up at stars not ceilings.

In the dim light of a million twinkling lights and a moon playing hide and seek behind fleeting clouds, she could see bats flying, darting to and fro between the treetops. Occasionally one would swoop down, diving at the insects flying above the fire, only to disappear just as quickly into the circle of darkness that enclosed the camp.

The barking sound of an irritated owl carried through the trees. In the circle of black velvet around the camp, animals moved through the underbrush. The fragrance of damp moss blended with the sweetness of late-blooming flowers at the water's edge and drifted over them.

She looked at Dan as he stirred in his sleep. He groaned when he moved his knee. Was she wrong? Did they have time to wait until his leg was better to travel?

His comments about the plane nagged at her. What had gone wrong? At first light she intended to find out. She had to prove to Dan that this wasn't her fault. Not that what he thinks should matter, she thought, punching her jacket into a temporary pillow. *He's not a pilot. He doesn't know anything about what it takes to fly up here.*

It shouldn't matter what Dan thought, but she admitted that it did. She wanted him to respect her as a pilot and as a woman. She was drawn not only to his intellect but also to his body. The memory of running her hands over his tight athletic form made her fingertips tingle. Beneath his flannel shirt, muscles had rippled under her probing fingers like the firm ridges left by the ocean tide in hard packed sand. His slim waist gave way to narrow hips and lean thighs. Sinewy thighs where her hands had lingered longer than necessary.

Craving began deep at the center of her body and spread outward, rushing toward a desire she had never experienced.

It was disgusting the way her body responded to Dan, especially when she didn't even know him. She used a mental crowbar and pried his image from her mind. Before she could think about him, or them, they had to get out of here alive. Tired and sore, she yanked the sleeping bag up around her ears. The heat of renewed anger at whatever had landed them in this situation would help keep the night chill at bay.

AJ had a pretty good idea Jorgensen was behind their crash and prove it she would.

CHAPTER THREE

At daybreak AJ threw back her sleeping bag and slipped into the trees to freshen up. They had to get moving. Early morning light filtered through the trees and danced across her eyes. Through the huge old trunks, she could see mist drifting above the lake. There was work to do, and no daylight to waste.

Dan was going to need support to walk. Close to camp she found a newly fallen branch that still had a bit of green in it. She pulled her pocketknife from her jacket and sat down on a log damp with dew to whittle the smaller branches from the main stem. At the top, she broke off two larger branches. Dan would need something to help him walk, and she'd be too busy with the packs and maps to do him much good. AJ tested out the crutch putting her full weight on it. Satisfied with her endeavor, she sneaked back into camp.

She approached Dan, her movements silenced by the natural cushion beneath her feet. Standing above him, she looked at his sleeping form. Peaceful features softened his face beneath wavy chestnut hair.

AJ stooped to his side. Regret for his pain and their predicament nagged her as she brushed his hair back from his eyes. She laid the back of her hand on his forehead checking for fever but found none. With a gentle smile, she set the branch down, so he couldn't fail to see it if he awakened before she came back from the wreckage of her plane.

She rose and placed a pot of coffee over the fire to brew. The aroma of fresh perked grounds soon filled the air. Two cups sat on a rock beside the fire ring. Procrastinating, AJ checked the camp for a third and fourth time dreading the moment when she would see her plane in the bright morning light. She had done everything she needed to.

With a wistful sigh, she looked through the trees for a moment longer before moving into them. Along the way, she looked at flowers and plants, stopped to listen to the sound of bullfrogs and crickets at the lake, the scurry of small birds and furry critters in the underbrush. A city person would find the different sounds oppressive if not threatening. They would be unknown and frightening to someone used to the sounds of city traffic.

Catching a slight movement in her peripheral vision, AJ stopped and watched a doe and her family. They returned her attention by watching with raised heads as her path came close to their browsing area. The late spring fawns might have been cast in bronze. A yearling male more curious than frightened twitched its ears in her direction as did the doe.

Sunlight slipped between pine boughs and hit her in the face. She moved on and the animals did the same. In the quiet of the post-dawn morning, it was impossible to imagine this had been the scene of a crash just hours earlier.

A gap grew in the trees as she entered the deep rut created by her plane the day before. Several yards down the path, she stopped and remembered the tearing sound of metal and the smell of dust and smoke. AJ looked at the twisted and partially burned hull as moisture filled her eyes. She silently cursed herself for being a sentimental fool. It didn't work. Memories flowed through her of the flights she had taken in this bird before her mother died.

AJ thought she would always have this plane to fly and to feel close to her mother in. Now it was gone. A dry sob burst from her lips. Slowly she drew a trembling breath into her chest. As she had when she lost her mother, AJ must wait to grieve, provided she and Dan made it out of the wilderness.

You have a responsibility to Dan. You have to get him out of this.

Remembering the past and crying over lost memories wasn't going to get them far. Refusing to let her tears spill over, she forced her attention to her present situation and straightened up, squaring her shoulders as she stiffened her back. She wiped her eyes on a wadded up, soggy tissue, then crammed it into a damp lump in her hip pocket. Abruptly, she turned to what remained of the storage compartment to grab a tool kit.

The engine cover had been ripped back, and she was able to squeeze under it to examine what was left of the plane's engine. Her feet slipped from their perch and a memory flashed through her mind. A picture of a little girl in faded coveralls, a greasy rag hanging from her hip pocket as she balanced on the edge of the plane, watching Charlie work on the engine. That little girl carried tools in her pockets, not dolls. She had not outgrown dogging after Charlie. Watching the Scotsman work on the planes was a favorite pastime in her teen years, the same torn and tattered rag hanging from her pocket to signal her occupation with mechanical things.

Among her predominantly male friends, she was "just one of the guys." She realized that hadn't bothered her until now. AJ shrugged and refocused her attention on the pile of crumpled metal in front of her.

Sunlight glanced off a piece of broken glass, drawing her attention to a timing device fastened near the radio wires. Knowing what was required to stall an engine and throw a pilot off course, she quickly located the same kind of devices by the magnetos and compass. Why hadn't she seen them in the pre-flight check?

she wondered. AJ answered her own question—because a pilot didn't normally look for sabotage.

Jorgensen! Damn his selfish hide.

He must have tampered with the plane before she left home. AJ couldn't think of anyone else that would retaliate in such a way. Cursing the man she felt was responsible for the sabotage, she removed the remaining bits of evidence.

"I'll see you behind bars for this." AJ thumped her hand against the fuselage, then went back to work, her anger fueling her moves.

As she finished, something large scuffled noisily up behind her. She hit her head on a tree limb as she jerked from under the bent engine cover. Scowling, AJ rubbed her head with her forearm, being careful not to drop the pieces of evidence cradled in her hands. She looked at the man who limped up to her using the makeshift crutch.

"Morning, AJ. Find anything?"

The deep timbre of his voice caressed her. Her movement arrested for a moment. His amused smile sparked off the golden flecks in his eyes. Her heart fluttered, stomach clutched. *What is it about him that turns me inside out?*

"Aurora?"

She realized he was watching her, the light of humor dancing in his eyes. Drawing herself back to reality with a jolt, she straightened away from the plane, the parts still in her greasy hands.

Dan looked up where she balanced on a stump to work on the plane. He laughed at her bringing a perplexed look to her face.

"Let me help you. Lean down here." He reached into a hip pocket, drew out a bandanna and proceeded to wipe her face and the end of her upturned nose being careful to avoid her injured forehead. "Grease," he said, holding the soiled cloth so she could see it.

"Thanks."

He sent her the genuine smile she was quickly coming to look for, the one with the ability to send her world into an inverted loop. Folding the dirty side in, he put the cloth back into his pocket.

"Find anything?" he asked again, snapping her out of her trance.

"You bet I did. I told you this wasn't my fault."

"I didn't mean to imply that it was."

"Never mind. It's not important." She jumped down and landed at his side, her arm brushing his. AJ scooted away to put distance between their bodies.

Dan frowned at the pile of junk in her hands. "What's that?" He nodded at the melted wire and glass fragments she held on her open palms.

"Evidence. I'm taking this back with me. Somebody put timing devices in there that would disable the engine and radio, as well as altering the compass readings. They made certain we'd crash, and that we couldn't get off a mayday. By sending us off course, he made it harder for us to find our way out or for search parties to locate us."

"Who on earth would want to hurt you?"

"What makes you think they were after me? You're a pretty high powered business type, aren't you?"

"That I might be," he said shaking his head, "but I don't do the kind of business that would have someone trying to get rid of me. The closest we get to intrigue is corporate espionage where another company sends in someone to steal our designs. Besides, nobody who might to get at me knows anything about your company. Only my parents know all the details of this trip."

"Well," she sighed, "that's pretty much what I figured, but it was worth a shot. If no one is after you, I think I know who did this. A man named Jorgensen."

"Who's he?"

"A creep who stole from my dad and some of our neighbors. I ran him off the property, and he was really angry when he left. He's desperate to stay out of jail." She frowned. "He's the only one I can think of who is slimy enough to do a thing like this."

"Why you? Surely there are others who are bringing charges against him."

"I'm spearheading a committee to bring joint charges and law suits against him." She glanced at the crumpled pile of memories wrapped up in the wreckage. "That son of a bitch! He's going to pay for this," she promised.

"That settles that question, and I agree completely. He's not going to get away with this kind of deal, but if we don't get out of this, no one will know what happened to us or who did it."

"We'll get out of here, Dan. I'll get back one way or another 'cause I'm going to see him behind bars. Let's go back to camp." AJ started to turn away, but Dan caught her arm and pulled her back around. She raised a questioning glance to his strong face.

"One suggestion?"

"Sure," she answered.

"Leave a note hidden in the plane that tells what you think happened and where we're going, in case we don't get out of this and someone finds the plane later. That way he'll at least be investigated for this even if we aren't around to see it."

"That's a good idea. I'll put today's date on it so they know when we started out."

She set down the stuff in her hands and wiped them on her old blue bandanna. Reaching into the smashed cockpit, she found a paper and pencil in what remained of the console.

When she was finished writing, she looked around the cockpit for a place to put the note. Knowing the headset and radio would be thoroughly checked out, she slipped the paper inside one of the broken ear pieces and turned to Dan.

"There. That ought to do it. Let's go."

This time when she turned for the camp, Dan didn't stop her, but limped along behind her.

They moved slowly through the trees as AJ deliberately checked her impatience to accommodate Dan's halting gait. She was eager to get underway. The sooner they made it back, the sooner she'd see Jorgensen arrested. She was determined to link the timing devices to Jorgensen one way or another. When they reached the camp, she laid the evidence on her pack.

She walked to Dan as she wiped her hands on the faded bandanna again, then taking his hands in hers, AJ helped him ease himself down onto a log by the dying campfire. She could see the thin film of perspiration that covered his face before it evaporated in the cool morning air. He shivered as a chill sped through his body. Lines of pain were sculpted deeply in his face, although he voiced no complaints.

"Are you all right, Dan?" At his nod, she continued, "Coffee?"

"Sure. Black is fine," he added out of habit.

"Black?" She chuckled. "You're not at the Ritz, you know. For the next week or two we're going to be living on boiled water and dehydrated food that has the taste and texture of a cheap sponge."

"Sorry. I forgot."

She handed him a mug of steaming liquid and two of the pain pills from their medical kit. At his questioning glance she simply gave him a firm look. "Take them." She softened her order with a smile.

Dan sipped the hot coffee and looked at her over the edge of his tin cup. "When are we going?"

Her gaze locked on his. "How's your leg? Can we get a few miles in today, or do you want to wait a day?"

"No, I'm ready. We may have to go slowly, but I'll stay with you as well as I can."

Tossing out the dregs of her coffee, AJ stood up. "All right, then. I'll finish stowing what we can take with us. Keep your leg up while you can. We're going to have to baby it for several days. Do you have anything in your pack like medicine or anything you can't live without?"

He smiled, a charming, sheepish smile. "Can we fit in my razor?"

AJ laughed.

"Now don't do that. I'm not vain. I can't stand a scratchy beard. When I was younger my buddies used to kid me. They thought it was sacrilegious to go on an all-male camping trip and not get scruffy. I never could stand that part of it. The razor's just a light disposable one." He sounded like a boy negotiating for candy.

She sent him a resigned look and shook her head. "Right. I'll find it. Do you want to go through your clothes, or shall I get what you'll need?"

"You go ahead."

"Okay. I'll be done in a few minutes."

At the plane, AJ unzipped the duffel bag Dan used and found neatly folded, outdoor clothing. She started digging through the methodical stacks to find two complete sets for him.

Under a couple of flannel shirts, she came across a folded Chicago Bears sweatshirt. When she pulled it out of the bag to add it to the pile, Dan's scent drifted to her. Stopping for a moment, she held the soft fleece fabric to her cheek, drawing in the spicy essence of after-shave from its folds. His image materialized as soon as the fragrance assaulted her senses.

Thrusting the shirt aside, she dug deeper in the bag. When she pulled a pair of black briefs from the bottom, she easily pictured his lean taut hips surrounded by the skimpy underwear. The skin on her face flushed with heat, and she quickly tossed the briefs onto the other clothes. Chiding herself for what she saw as a cheap and tawdry response, AJ forced herself to focus on collecting his things without further speculation on what he would look like in them.

A short time later they were ready to head south. The thick down sleeping bags they used the night before were left behind and replaced by lightweight backpacking gear instead. She added a small first aid kit, dehydrated food, plastic water canteens, aluminum cookware, and assorted necessities.

"Ready, Dan?"

"You bet."

"I think we're east of Missisa Lake, closer to James Bay. We're going to head south to Albany River, and then we can follow it east to Fort Albany or Kashechewan."

As she leaned over to help him to his feet, he caught her wrist with his large hand. His thumb rested where her pulse throbbed. Surprised at being caught by him, her gaze flew to meet his, a silent unspoken question easy to read in her brilliant blue eyes. Mesmerized, her gaze stayed locked with his as he pulled her onto her knees in front of him. His free hand slowly came up to rest along her jaw, the warm large fingers resting under her chin, caressing her throat. His thumb traced slow circles on her cheek. AJ's heart hammered so hard, she knew it must be thundering through the virgin forest.

Slowly, deliberately, he pulled her face to his to claim her lips with his. The gentle pressure grew and became demanding, urging her lips apart so their mouths joined in a flood of sensation. Reluctant to end the moment, but knowing she must, AJ forced herself back to reality.

"What was that for?"

"You're quite a woman, Miss MacKenzie." He set her away slightly and smiled into her eyes.

Embarrassed, she braced her hands against his thighs and pushed herself to her feet.

"We'd better get moving," she said. A husky voice reached

her ears that didn't sound anything like her own. Her lips trembled in anticipation of another taste of his. She would have sworn her toes curled in her hiking boots. Fear mixed with need. Wanting warred with self-control.

"You look like a rabbit caught in the headlights of a car. Why?" he whispered. "Why are you afraid of me, Aurora?"

She studied the lines furrowing his forehead. "I don't have summer flings, Dan. I'm not a one-night stand, and you and I are from two different worlds. A brief affair is all we could have with any success, and I'm not prepared to accept that."

Dan stuffed his hands in his coat pockets. "All right, AJ. I appreciate your candor, but I don't agree that our worlds are so far apart. I won't let you run from me forever. Now, help me up, and we'll get out of here." His serious tone fled as he pulled a plastic package out of his pocket. He gave her a silly grin. "Wintergreen?"

AJ managed to choke a response past the lump in her throat. "Sure," she croaked, taking one of the thick, pink, powdery rounds and slipping it into her mouth. She wondered at the ease with which he could change subjects. It was as easy for him as a chameleon changing colors.

A slight smile brought a dimple to his left cheek. "It looks as though we're going to vacation together after all."

His smile brought laugh lines to his eyes, and she was forced to match it with one of her own as she pulled him to his feet. This flight was getting more interesting by the moment.

CHAPTER FOUR

Late in the day, AJ eased Dan down to sit on a log. "How are you?"

"Hanging in there."

His gray features belied his words. "Let's take about twenty minutes, then get a little farther before dark." She dropped her pack beside him and pulled her compass from her pocket to take another reading.

"Any chance your dad might have tried to contact us? Maybe they're looking after all." Dan ran his fingers through his hair, then rested his forearms on his thighs.

"I hope not."

Dan swung toward her, confusion clear on his features.

"I don't mean exactly that. It would be nice if someone was already looking, but if Dad knows I've gone down..." She shook her head slowly, pain twisting her gut. "I don't know how he'd go through this again."

"Again?"

"My mother and he went down, and she died in the crash. He was on the waiting end that time, waiting for rescue." A heavy sigh slipped from her chest. She couldn't bear the thought of causing him such pain a second time. "I'm just not sure how well he'd handle the news that I'd crashed."

"Most people are a lot stronger than we think. I'm sure he'll be fine. And the sooner someone finds us, the sooner we'll all be okay."

"I know, but I really hope we make it to a radio before he finds out we're down."

She thought of the pain her father had experienced losing his wife. Loving and losing, it was something AJ had no intention of risking. She moved away from Dan and sat down to rest a few minutes before they moved on. The sooner they were back, the sooner he'd head to Chicago, and out of her life—where he belonged.

Fear for his daughter engulfed Roy MacKenzie as he stared into his coffee mug; the contents of it long since grown cold. Red checkered curtains lifted in the afternoon breeze that blew off the lake and filtered through the partially open kitchen window. He slumped in his wheelchair, the forest green material of his cowl-necked sweater wrapped tightly around his neck to ward off a chill. His shoulders sagged. The mussed state of his hair highlighted gray streaks in the fading red and he appeared far older than his fifty-one years.

He listened intently, catching every nuance of the conversation going on five feet from him. The logo on the cup in his hand caught his gaze and drew his attention from the other man's voice. A white biplane did a loop against a background of deep blue. AJ had designed it for him when they changed the company's name to Sky Dancer.

AJ was a natural flyer. As much as he hated seeing her doing stunts, Roy had to admit that. The aerobatics came as easily to her as leaping does to a cougar. Even so, his confidence in her ability couldn't stop the fear that clutched his heart as he watched, and waited. He would only be satisfied when she was safely back on the lake.

A grunt from across the room drew his attention back into the cozy kitchen. A crackling fire on the worn stone hearth had taken the morning chill off the room.

The red-haired mechanic paced back and forth at the end of the phone cord. Still in coveralls, the ever-present greasy rag hanging from his hip pocket, he clutched the phone to his ear. He, too, seemed to have aged overnight. Charlie's frown was etched into granite features. He stopped pacing and stood twisting the phone cord around and around his fingers.

"Yeah... Okay. I'll get back to you in a few minutes. I have to talk to Roy. Thanks." He gently replaced the receiver with a tired sigh, silent for a moment before slowly turning.

"What'd they say, Charlie?"

"It's a good thing you wanted to talk to her..."

Fear closed his throat but he had to ask. "Because?"

"Nobody has seen any sign of the plane at either lake, and no one's had any better luck than us at raising them on the radio. You want me to send someone up to check out the lakes?"

Roy lowered his chin to his chest and sighed as his worst fears were confirmed. There was a very real possibility that his daughter was lost in the forests of northern Canada. Engrossed in his private thoughts for only seconds, he lifted his head as he set his jaw.

"No, we're going. I'll get a call in to Satterfield Senior and let him know they may have had trouble. We're going to need another plane. I think *Northern Flights* was finished for the season. Call Ben and see if he can get over here and fly us up there. We'll have to fly to Thunder Bay tonight, then we'll go north at first light." He drew a shuddering breath.

"It'll be okay, Roy. She's the best pilot around. If they had trouble, she's put the plane down somewhere to work on it."

"I had a feeling there'd be trouble this time. I should have insisted on her not going."

Charlie laughed. "You really believe you can tell her what to do anymore now than you could when she was a sky-happy kid?"

A smile crept over Roy's strained features. The lines of worry eased slightly. "No, I don't suppose I can. Anyway, maybe this will be a wild goose chase." He shook his head. "Normally I can get her on the radio when she's out like this. Something's not right, I'm sure of it. Get on the other phone, and I'll use this one to call Satterfield's people."

A buzzer interrupted Geoffrey Satterfield's work. He reached across a stack of papers and slapped down the intercom button. Irritated with the intrusion, his voice was sharper than he intended.

"Yes, Miss Taylor. What is it?"

"Mr. MacKenzie on line two, and he says it's urgent."

"MacKenzie? I don't know anyone by that name."

"I know, sir. He says it has to do with your son...and it's very important. He..."

Puzzled and curious, he cut her off and snapped up the phone. An uneasy feeling began in the pit of his stomach as he answered the call.

"Geoffrey Satterfield here. Who is this?"

"Roylas MacKenzie. My company flew your son to Canada two days ago. I'm afraid we may have a problem."

Dread slammed into Satterfield's midsection as he listened to the sentence every parent fears he will one day hear. The knuckles on his hand turned white as he clasped the phone to his ear. Daniel. If anything had happened to... Choking aside the fear that gripped him, he spoke into the receiver with deadly calm.

"What sort of problem?" he asked, straightening in the leather chair, automatically reaching for a pen and blank paper.

"There's no need to be alarmed, at least not yet, but I want you to be aware we haven't been able to make contact with the pilot. My mechanic and I are flying to Thunder Bay today. We'll go on at first light and should be able to let you know by tomorrow afternoon whether they made the lake or not."

"Why do you think they might have had trouble and not just lost their radio communication? What kind of plane are they in?" He never gave Roy a chance to answer. "How experienced was the pilot you sent him with?" This time he waited for a response.

"AJ's been flying since the age of twelve and is extremely capable."

"How many years has he been flying?"

A heavy silence crossed the phone line, then Roy sighed and answered. "*She*, Mr. Satterfield. AJ's my daughter. She's been at it fourteen years, and is one of the best pilots up here. There's no need to be concerned on that score, and the plane was in top condition. I'll be in touch tomorrow."

"No." Satterfield took control of himself and the situation. No emotion slid into his voice to indicate the terror he felt at the thought that something had happened to his only son. "No," he repeated. "I'm coming up. I'll meet you in Thunder Bay."

"It might take you some time to get a flight up there," Roy said.

Satterfield snorted. "I'll come in the company jet. I'll be there before you are. Call me at the Hilton when you get in. Good-bye, Mr. MacKenzie." He abruptly hung up.

Roy stared at the dead receiver, muttering under his breath about not needing this kind of help.

Charlie hurried into the kitchen as Roy replaced the instrument in its cradle. "What'd you find out?"

"Besides the fact that Mr. Satterfield Senior sounds like a pain in the ..." Roy stopped, shook his head, continued. "He's going to meet us in Thunder Bay and go on with us in the morning. Is Ben coming?"

"You couldn't keep him away. He'll be here soon."

"Good. Let's get moving then. Go pack what you'll need for a few days."

Swinging his chair around, Roy moved down the hall to gather what he would need. As he rolled past AJ's room, Roy stopped and looked inside. The bed was neatly made and stacked with overstuffed pillows in bright colors. Colors of the northern lights like those he could see in her hair on a bright sunny day.

The walls were papered with posters of historic biplanes doing stunts or carrying wing walkers. Over her bed was an enlargement of his favorite photograph. It had been taken of AJ and her grandfather sky dancing shortly before his death. What if she's gone? He shook his head in silent refusal. She'd be fine. She had to be. Roy gently closed her door and continued down the hall to his own room while Charlie slipped into the guest room to gather his things. A tear gathered in Roy's eye. It was just like AJ to get Charlie to stay with him while she was away. Always worrying about somebody else. He cleared his throat and got to work.

Roy quickly pulled clothing from already messy drawers. What kind of a man was their client? Could he count on the passenger to watch out for his girl? The man seemed too citified to be much use in the woods. He thought of the father, Daniel Satterfield. *Kind of high and mighty if you ask me.* Roy humphed and dug deeper into his drawer.

AJ turned in time to see Dan stagger. He grunted then swore quietly. She quickly noted his pallor, his face dotted with beads of perspiration.

"Break time." She dropped her packs and moved to help Dan ease his body onto a log. "How you doin'?" she asked softly.

"Swell, just marvelous."

"We'll slow down."

"No, I'm sorry. I'm doing all right, really. I just tweaked my knee. How far have we come?"

"Not far. We're moving slowly, but we'll get there. Don't worry about it. We'll rest a few minutes then go on for a while."

"AJ?"

"Hmm?"

"Anybody besides me ever tell you, you're an unbelievable lady?"

A chuckle slipped from her before she could stop it. He looked wounded when she rebuffed his compliment. Sorry for hurting his feelings, she hurried to soften her

response. "Is that because I can make a pretty good pine needle mattress or because I can cook over a campfire?"

"I'm serious, Aurora."

A shiver slipped through her as it did every time he wrapped his voice around her name.

"You are stronger, more self-confident than any woman I've ever met. Most of the women I know would have had a screaming fit by now. They certainly wouldn't be calmly leading me through the wilderness with a half-assed map and a compass."

An embarrassed flush heated her face. "It's not half-assed. It's just a flight map instead of a topographical map. And I think you might be surprised at how competent those other women would be given similar circumstances. Besides, if I was lost in Chicago or had a broken-down car in a bad neighborhood, you can bet I'd be the one having hysteria."

Dan looked into her calm eyes. "I doubt that. I really do."

Her heart slammed against her ribs—slowly, methodically—at

his unexpected praise. Unable to think of a graceful answer, she jumped to her feet. "Come on. We won't get far this way." The heat of his palms registered as she helped him to his feet, and she dropped his hands to snatch her own away. A slow smile spread across his face as his gaze locked on hers. She spun away, hoping they were found soon. Resisting Dan was not going to be easy.

Roy MacKenzie met with the airport authorities and told them his concerns. They had already heard from Geoffrey Satterfield. Attempts to reach AJ by radio had been made again at Satterfield's insistence. The range stations at Nakina, Pagwa, and Ft. Albany all tried, but to no avail.

Roy told the airport authorities of his plan to fly to Missisa Lake to check on AJ and Dan. He asked them to be ready to institute a search if he couldn't find his daughter. Reluctant to sit and wait, but realizing the futility of going north in the dark, he returned to his hotel and called the Hilton.

"Satterfield?"

"Yes."

"Roy MacKenzie. I just came from the airport. We'll head out at 6:00 a.m. Meet us at the small plane terminal."

"My pilot will take the lead on this—"

"Your pilot doesn't know Canada. Ben does. I'll see you in the morning."

Roy abruptly hung up cutting off further discussion and rolled into the bedroom. They needed an early night. He wanted to be in the air at daybreak.

The sun topped the trees as the plane carrying the three men leveled off. Roy handed Satterfield a pair of binoculars as they approached Lake Nipigon.

"Keep your eyes peeled for any reflection of light or a flash of red and white paint. We'll drop down and cruise over the lake, but I doubt that AJ would have set down this close to Thunder Bay without someone noticing them in three days," Roy said. "Ben, I didn't thank you yesterday for coming so quick."

The pilot shook his head. "We were finished for the season at *Northern Flights*, and you know you couldn't keep me away even if we hadn't been."

Roy nodded and returned to scanning the ground for any sign of AJ's plane.

Ben swooped down, then straightened out only feet above the surface of the lake. He flew the shoreline following every inlet and every curve. AJ's plane wasn't tucked beneath the aging coniferous giants. Ben swung the plane away from the lake and resumed his previous altitude.

During the flight, every flicker of light, every strange shadow and shape was checked out. Whenever one of the men spotted a reflection, Ben skimmed the treetops. Time and again Roy shifted from initial relief that they had not found a crash site to disappointment in not finding his daughter.

Ben's new Beaver was fast. A short time later they were circling over Missisa Lake. There was no sign of a campsite nor was anyone fishing from the shore.

A feeling of despair began to grip Roy as he accepted the idea that something had happened to force AJ to crash land somewhere in this wild country. The trees packed as tightly as penguins on an ice floe. There was no chance the plane could be landed intact if they hadn't come across a lake.

The picture of AJ's plane slammed into a hulking tree, trapping her, finishing her young life was almost too much for Roy to bear. He'd been through that once. Damned if he'd let it happen again. Roy shook his head. *Like I can control destiny*.

During the flight, Satterfield remained stoic, saying nothing except to point out a suspicious spot in the trees. He simply stared out at the trees, sliding his binoculars methodically back and forth across the terrain seemingly absorbed in the task.

Ben broke the silence. "Where now, Roy?"

"Maybe they decided to go on to Opinnagua. Let's head up there to check it out."

"Right," Ben said. He banked the plane to the right and headed farther north across the Canadian countryside.

When they reached Opinnagua, Ben circled tightly to keep the plane over the lake as his passengers searched for any sign of the plane or the people it had carried.

"Anybody see anything?" Roy asked. He was met with silence and solemn head shaking. "Set her down, Ben. We need a quick break to reconnoiter."

Ben brought the plane down in a smooth landing, then taxied to the shore. He climbed down first and jumped to the ground from the pontoon. Roy watched Satterfield refuse his help and land on the earth with a thud. Ben shook his head as Roy let him lift him clear of the plane and onto the small beach.

Satterfield paced in short quick strides. His shoulders were square and rigid, his jaw clenched. Obviously impatient with the delay, he quickly spoke up. "How much time do you intend to waste here, MacKenzie?"

"We'll only be here a few minutes, then we'll head back to the airport. Ben, get your maps and let's pick a likely course to follow back toward Thunder Bay. We may as well eliminate a search transect on the way in." Roy turned to Charlie. "Get a hold of the range stations. Give them the info and tell them we're sure they've gone down, or they would be at their destination by now."

Roy issued orders as adrenaline surged through his veins. "Ask them to contact the Canadian Civil Air Patrol to get ready for a search and rescue operation between Missisa Lake and Thunder Bay."

They had to find her, just had to. He didn't think he could bear the loss of another member of his family. To lose any of his children was unthinkable, but Aurora Jean. She was more than his child, she was his partner, his soul mate. The hours they spent in a cockpit sharing their common love of flying were the most special hours he spent with anyone except his Annie Jean.

Lost in thought, Roy jerked to attention when Ben jumped off the pontoon and landed at his feet, flight maps in hand. They opened the ones covering the territory from Opinnagua to Thunder Bay.

"What do you think, Roy? If she was having trouble, where would she go?" Ben asked.

After studying maps that he essentially knew by heart, Roy turned a determined gaze on the young pilot.

"Ogoki. The Albany River is pretty wide there, and there are radios and people all year."

"MacKenzie," the smooth tenor of Satterfield's voice rang out, the slightest hint of desperation slipping into it. "Why wouldn't she send a mayday or get a radio signal off? Didn't the plane have homing devices for an emergency like this?"

"The plane's radio must be out. Probably the transponder, too, or we'd be receiving it."

Roy looked carefully at the executive for the first time. On the surface he saw a self-sufficient, autocratic, pain in the ass. Looking closer, he realized they were much more alike than he'd expected. Satterfield might have been trying to appear in command, but the rapidly flicking fingertips, fingertips that were colorless, gave away his inner turmoil. His closed demeanor had kept Roy from trying to reach him.

"Look," Roy said, "we got off to a bad start. I know you're as concerned about your son as I am my daughter. You should know that AJ is special. She's level headed and experienced."

"But," Satterfield began.

Roy held up a hand to cut him off.

"I'm sure she just had to set the plane down and is waiting for us to find her. We'll locate them. It's only a matter of time." Roy spoke confidently to bolster himself as much as Satterfield.

Geoffrey appeared to consider him for only a moment. He nodded his agreement as he pulled in a long drag of air. "Let's go. We've got a lot of territory to cover before dark."

CHAPTER FIVE

The harsh jangle of the phone shattered the quiet in Jorgensen's darkened room. From under an apricot satin comforter, he groped for the switch on the bedside lamp. Soft light flooded the room a moment before the receiver was snatched from its cradle. Light bounced off a ring of fiery rubies and diamonds. The image of the burning wings of a phoenix set in white gold reflected from one of his fingers catching his attention as his fingers closed over the silver phone.

"Who is this?"

"It's me, Mr. Jorgensen."

Instantly awake, he shoved the cover aside and reached for his glasses. "What the hell do you want at this hour? It better be important."

Before the answer could come across the lines, he was on his feet, pacing beside the chrome frame of his bed. The phone cord twisted around his fingers when he reached up to tweak his glasses.

"I know I'm not supposed to bother you, but I thought this was important," a voice whined.

"All right, all right. Spit it out! What's the problem?"

"MacKenzie knows his daughter and her client are missing. He's already headed to Thunder Bay to lead a search for her. I found out something else, too."

As the breath whooshed out of his body, Jorgensen slumped onto the mussed bed. His fingers twitched as thoughts whirled through his mind. It didn't matter. They couldn't have survived the crash. He had seen to that. Sylvester was just a nervous twit.

"What?" he asked, his voice deadly quiet.

"That client of hers, Satterfield?"

"What about him?"

"He's rich and comes from a really powerful family in Chicago. His old man is connected to some big politicians."

As he finished, the man's voice rose an octave.

"Calm down. I'll handle it." Jorgensen spoke into the receiver slowly, deliberately. The other voice continued to whine, the pitch of it rising steadily.

"What are we gonna do?"

"I said I'll handle it," Jorgensen snapped. "Don't call me again." He slammed the phone down and jumped up to pace across the steel gray carpet. Glass and chrome furniture sparkled in the dim light from the bedside table. No one was going to bring him down. No one. He'd see to that.

He crossed the room again and dropped down at a small desk. Picking up the phone. He glanced at the clock and saw it was only three AM. When a groggy voice answered, he issued orders to his pilot. "Have my jet ready at six." The grave tone of his voice spoke volumes. "I'm flying to Canada at daybreak to help look for a friend that's been lost in a plane crash. I couldn't live with myself if I didn't do everything I can to help."

He replaced the receiver, chuckling as he moved back to the bed and piled the pillows against the headboard. Leaning back against it, he lit the tip of a thin cigar and pulled smoke into his lungs.

Who would suspect I had anything to do with the crash if I'm on hand to help find the body of my lost neighbor? He'd be properly distraught over the tragic death of the flyer when he happened to be the one to locate the body, he decided. And that old fool MacKenzie and his nosy mechanic... *I can be as sympathetic as anyone.* His lips curved around the cigar as he congratulated himself on his foresight.

AJ awoke wrapped in a space-age sleeping bag. Made for backpacking, it was designed to provide the most warmth with the least amount of weight. The results were perfect, but she felt like she was sleeping in aluminum foil. Five days of waking up in it were about three too many.

The sleeping bag was pulled around her head and ears, only her face sticking out in the chill morning air. Her breath came in short little spurts. Across from her, on the far side of the remains of the fire, lay Dan. The sun danced on his wavy hair highlighting the flashes of gold mixed in with chestnut. Pounding against her ribs, her heart rate escalated as it always did when she looked too long at him. Her gaze traveled up and down the sleeping bag while she silently wished she could see the well-muscled body beneath.

The thought was an unusually bold one for her, and she felt the heat rising in her face. When her gaze came back to his face, she was startled to find his eyes wide open, a lazy smile spreading across his features.

He knew exactly what she had been thinking. Her face burned. To cover her embarrassment she threw a "Good morning" at him, then climbed out of her sleeping bag, grabbed her jacket, and walked into the woods.

The dew had frozen turning to frost on the organic carpet. It crunched under her feet reminding them an early winter could catch them at any time. Nearby a brook bubbled over boulders. Above the sound of the effervescent water came the gnawing sound of a beaver whittling away at a tree in the distance.

As she moved between the trees, AJ was thankful for the early morning chill that cooled her overheated features. The fresh warm sun hit in patches and was already melting the frost to cover the pine duff and sparse grass with heavy dew. To slow her rapidly beating heart, she breathed deeply taking in the damp, sweet smell of the forest. Muttering to herself about the possibility of having lost her power to reason, AJ disappeared into the brush carrying the towel, canteen, and toothbrush she had grabbed as she dashed from the camp.

When she came back to start breakfast, Dan was gone. She assumed he had gone down by the lake to shave. The cellophane crinkled as she ripped open a package of dehydrated food to pour mustard colored powder into a small cup. Adding water from a canteen, she absently stirred the mix with a fork wondering what Dan was doing to take so long.

AJ poured liquid eggs into a pan and set it beside the fire to cook as she waited impatiently for his return. She watched the eggs gel into lumps, before she stirred the unappetizing mess sticking to her pan.

Yuck. I'll never eat dehydrated food again when we get out of here.

Fifteen minutes passed, breakfast was long since done and the remains grown cold. Still he didn't return. AJ began to picture all of the things that can go wrong in the wilderness and started to worry. Thinking that perhaps his leg had given out on him, she left the pan with his breakfast warming by the rekindled fire and walked down to the lake.

Her father had taught her to move quietly in the forest and she did so now not knowing what she might find. She stopped as a flash of golden skin caught her attention through the few scrubby bushes growing between the huge conifers. Blushing, she turned away to head back into the trees. Something stopped her.

Reluctant, she gave in to curiosity and turned back to look toward the lake. AJ knew she should leave, but she was drawn forward, one unconscious step at a time. She knew it was wrong, but she was compelled to move forward on silent steps.

At the edge of the clearing, she stopped and watched as Dan limped across the beach and entered the icy lake. He drew in a sharp breath as the chilled water rushed over his warm flesh. His clothes—all of them—were hanging on a bush. She caught her breath and bit down on her lip to swallow the startled sound that tried to escape from her lips. Unable to take her eyes from his sculpted form, she raised a shaking hand to her face, a face she knew without question was fire engine red.

Dan dove under the water, then surfaced holding a bar of soap he must have taken from his pack. He lathered his face and arms, then stood waist deep in the water. AJ watched as he ran the soap over his chest. A shiver raced through him as the chill air hit the water beaded on his body. Apparently not wanting to linger, he quickly ran the bar of soap over the ripply muscles that were covered by a fine mat of curly hair. Her gaze followed the hand that held the soap as it moved down across his abdomen where the hair grew in a darker vee before disappearing into the water. The reddish blond hair stood out against his tanned chest.

What would it feel like to run her fingers over that tight rippled chest, to feel the texture of his curly hair, she wondered. What would it be like to be in the water with him, bare breast to bare chest?

Shocked at the turn her thoughts had taken, AJ caught herself up short and thought again that she should leave, but her feet seemed set in concrete. All she could do was stand and watch as he dove under to rinse off. As he went under, his shapely bare buttocks and solid thighs flashed in the morning light, and her mind registered the fact that he was tan all over.

The smooth surface broke gently as he stood again. Transfixed, she stared at him wanting to see all of his powerful male body. The morning sounds of the forest were lost to her. All she could hear was the incessant pounding of her pulse. She couldn't seem to move—until Dan looked straight at her.

He smiled suggestively, one eyebrow raised in a questioning arch. "Shall I stand up and finish, Aurora, or would you rather join me?"

AJ let out a gasp, spun around, and bolted into the forest like a frightened doe, mortified that she had been caught like a peeping Tom. She dodged through the trees and ran around occasional bushes that blocked her path. His deep laughter echoed across the water and through the forest.

When she reached camp, she collapsed on a log and drew in a shaky breath as she buried her face in her hands. *What on earth is the matter with me? That man has cost me every shred of dignity I ever had.*

She shook her head. It didn't matter anyway. A romance with him could never work. He'd be going back to Chicago after they returned to the states. As the only pilot for Sky Dancer, AJ couldn't possibly leave her home. The company was the only income her father had. Dan would go. She'd stay. There was no other way.

Her thoughts of his leaving were quickly overshadowed by her memory of what she had just done. Shattered by what she considered to be her own crude behavior, and worse by being caught at it, she steeled herself to face him when he returned. How could she possibly have done such a thing to a client? What must he think of her?

A short time later, Dan hobbled back into camp, his hair still damp, the natural waves curling slightly around his face and over his ears. He still used the walking stick, although he wasn't leaning on it as heavily as he had before. AJ immediately turned her back to him and fought to appear busy beside the fire. She pretended not to notice him as she scooped lukewarm leathery eggs onto a plate.

"AJ?" Dan moved toward her, his hand outstretched.

"Here." She ignored his questioning tone and shoved the plate into his hand, again turning her back.

"Look, AJ, I'm sorry. I didn't mean to embarrass you like that or to frighten you. I was only teasing. You have such a delightful way of flushing whenever you think about..."

"I get the point, and I'm not afraid of you." She snapped at him, angry with herself for being caught in such a humiliating position.

He out down the plate and held up his empty hand, palm out in a placating gesture.

"Okay. Fine. I'm just saying I'm sorry, that's all. You don't have to bite my head off."

AJ sighed. "I know. I'm the one who should apologize. I should have left when I saw what you were doing."

"What were you doing down there, anyway?"

AJ shrugged, her gaze lowered to the ground, so she couldn't look into his. "I got worried when you didn't come back. I was afraid your leg was giving you trouble or you'd met a bear or something. I really am sorry."

"Someday I hope to return the favor." She gasped at the sensual promise in his quiet statement, but failed to find any comment to make regarding his innuendo. Besides, what could she say to dispute his wish when the idea of it sent a shiver of glorious anticipation bounding through her own body. What would it be like to have him look at her in such an intimate way?

Dan chuckled at her horrified expression. "Don't worry about it, Aurora."

Her heart twisted as he stroked her name with his deep voice.

"Hadn't we better get going?" he asked. "We're wasting daylight."

"Right." AJ jumped up, thankful for the change of subject. "Hurry up and eat while I get things stowed away."

Dan chewed on a yellow re-hydrated sponge that passed as scrambled eggs. AJ caught the look of distaste that tugged the corners of his lips into a frown.

"Sorry, it's all we've got."

"Don't worry about it. It's better than bark. How far do you think we've come?"

"Maybe fifteen miles or so. Stopping to rest your leg really slows us down, but I'd rather do that than have you overdo it and get us stuck 'cause you can't walk at all."

"Are we still traveling on the same heading today?"

"Definitely. I want to keep moving toward the Albany River."

"Are you sure nobody's lookin' for us?" he asked between bites.

"I suppose it's possible," she shrugged. "Pop was pretty agitated about me making this trip alone, so he may have tried to radio me to be sure I was at Opinnagua. If he did and couldn't get us, then you can bet they're looking, but no one else would miss us."

"Right, well we'll just keep hikin' then."

"Listen, when we get to a good camp site tonight," she said, "we need to take time to do some fishing, and I should make some soup or something. We need fresh food. This dehydrated stuff is running low. I have about five more days of it left, if we're careful. I'd like to start supplementing it as much as possible in case we're out here longer than I thought we would be."

Dan dumped the last of his eggs off the tin plate and handed it to AJ before she finished closing her pack.

"Fresh food sounds great to me, but how do you plan to make soup?"

"Don't ask, just eat and enjoy!" She picked the pack up and slung it with practiced ease onto her back, then handed the smaller pack to Dan. "Come on, let's go."

They moved off slowly, conserving Dan's energy and trying to keep the pain in his leg to a minimum. Moving south, they used both the sun and the compass to stay on course. AJ frequently consulted the maps, but, without being certain of their starting point, she was not able to pinpoint their exact location on the map.

The ritual was more of a comforting reflex than anything. The forest was dotted with thousands of glacial lakes and streams, all of which began to look alike after a while. They moved around the lakes and marshes whenever possible, crossed the streams on logs or rocks, and waded only when necessary, trying to keep their clothing dry. Although each of them carried a dry set, they didn't want to take time to dry boots and clothes.

It was getting colder each night, and they couldn't afford to be stuck with two sets of wet clothing. For the past twenty-four hours, clouds had been building and even the daytime temperatures were falling. AJ kept a watchful eye on the sky afraid they were going to get the early taste of winter instinct told her was coming. If so, she knew some sort of shelter had to be found.

By mid afternoon, Dan was becoming tired and the lines etched on his face were evidence of the pain he was in. AJ called a halt for some much-needed rest. She knelt beside him to check his bandage and was shocked to see the flesh swollen against the fabric, cutting off the circulation to his lower leg.

"Why the devil didn't you tell me your leg was swelling up like this? Look at that! What happened? I thought it was better."

"It was. I slipped on the wet grass earlier and twisted it again."

"You must be in terrible pain. *And*, it serves you right! What is the matter with you?" She impulsively punched his chest nearly knocking him backward off the log.

Dan looked at her sheepishly. "I didn't want to slow us down."

"That's all well and good, but it won't mean diddly if you get gangrene and lose that leg. Lean back and let me take a look."

She gently released the tape and unwound the wraps, so she could get a good look at his knee. It was still black and blue and the skin was taut with the swelling. She left him and moved to a nearby spring-fed pool to dip a bandanna into the crystal clear, freezing water. Quickly she moved back and laid it over the swollen joint hoping to ease the tightness. She softly laid her hands over it, pressing gently. Large warm hands came down over hers. She caught her breath as a hot jolt of current raced through her body.

Her pulse roared in her ears sounding as though there was a large river with rapids nearby. Dan reached down and lifted her chin, so she was forced to look into his face. He was smiling at her, but his expression changed when fear reflected from her eyes.

His smile faded, as he bent down and pressed his lips to hers. Dan's mouth moved across hers, his tongue teasing her lips open. She raised up to meet him half way and rested her hands on his thighs for balance. His large, gentle hands spanned her waist, then slipped up her sides to pull her closer. The kiss deepened and she became lost in it—spiraling down, totally oblivious to her surroundings. Nothing mattered but the taste and feel of him.

Sensations spun through her body. She was lost.

So completely lost in his embrace, she only vaguely registered the snap and crackle of twigs that could only be caused by the cautious but steady approach of footsteps—heavy ones.

When she thought she would surely drown in the heavenly feelings evoked by the touch of his hands on her body, an angry bellow trumpeted across the small clearing. Breaking away from him, she spun around on her heels afraid of what she would see, but already having a pretty good idea what was behind them. She stared straight into the eyes of an infuriated, twelve hundred-pound female moose. Its ears flipped forward and back like rotating antennae for a moment before they were clamped to its thick neck. Dirt flew in all directions as it dug in the dirt like an enraged Brahma bull.

It charged toward them and stopped, shook its head, pawed the ground, and bellowed again. AJ looked over her shoulder and groaned when she saw the moose's calf behind them, peacefully grazing in the water, unaware that its mother was coming to its defense. They had unwittingly come between the two animals.

"Blast! I'm going to draw her away. When I run, you head into the forest away from her calf. Understand?" she said quietly.

"Wait! Don't do that!" He grabbed for her hand but missed. It was too late. She sprinted away, the moose right behind her pounding along in a gangly gallop, still furious and intent on running her over.

AJ ran as fast as she could, heading through the trees for cover. She darted from one to another as she looking for one she could climb before the animal caught up to her. Her breath came quick and hard, and she silently prayed for strength. The large creature closed in on her. She looked back over her shoulder.

That was a mistake. When she looked forward again, she found herself running straight toward ancient boards she knew crisscrossed a gaping hole. The aging wood was a faded gray color and showing signs of rot. She skidded to a halt, sliding on the slick pine needles in spite of the heavy tread on her hiking boots. Teetering on the edge of oblivion, she tried desperately to regain her footing. If she fell, the boards wouldn't hold her.

Rocking back and forth, she waved her arms to catch her balance. She regained her footing and sucked in a quick breath sighing a prayer of thanks as she balanced on the balls of her feet like a tennis pro, ready to dodge either direction around the hole. Before she could move, she was hit from behind by a mass of flesh and fur. When she hit the boards they shattered, showering pieces of rotted wood down on her as the moose slam-dunked her into the enveloping darkness.

AJ screamed as she fell, bouncing off the sides of the shaft, sending showers of dirt and rock free-falling to the bottom. Breath whooshed from her body as she slammed onto a ledge, her fall stopped at last. Looking up toward the light, she could see the moose peaking down into the darkness. An hysterical giggle escaped from her lips as she fought to pull air into her lungs.

She peered down into the hole, hoped to see dirt and saw instead—nothing, nothing but dark emptiness. She sank back against the shaft wall balanced on the edge of a black bottomless void.

CHAPTER SIX

Dan crashed through the trees using his crutch to bang against branches and brush. He yelled as loud as he could, trying to get the moose to go away. It worked and he watched the beast crash off through the trees toward her calf. His relief was short lived as fear of losing AJ snatched at his mind.

"AJ! Aurora, answer me!"

She answered slowly, sounding breathless. Dan peered into the darkness, but with the sun at his back, it was impossible to see more than her dark shape at the end of a long tunnel of darkness.

"Dan? Dan, help me!"

"All right. Stay calm, now. Are you hurt?"

"No, I don't think so. But I'm not at the bottom. I'm on a ledge, and I can't tell how deep this thing is. You've got to get me out." Her voice rose as she spoke.

"Hang on. I'm going to find something to reach down to you. Don't move," he ordered. "Stay perfectly still."

Panic gripped his body as he rushed to find what he needed. If he lost her, he might as well follow her to oblivion. That realization shocked him to his booted feet. He couldn't stay with her at Sky Dancer. He couldn't go back to Chicago alone. Maybe they could both hide out from reality and stay in Canada — together. His heart skipped and danced erratically as he wondered what would happen if she fell to the bottom of the chasm.

A cabin came into view as he raced down a worn path. He called out for help, but got no answer. Coiled rope lay on the faded wood porch. He grabbed it and hurried back as fast as his hobbling gait would allow.

When he returned he found her frantic.

"What took so long? Get me out of here!"

"All right, honey. Take it easy." He spoke in soothing tones trying to keep her calm. "There's a trail up here that leads to this shaft. I followed it to a small cabin and found a

rope. It's kind of odd, though. The thing looks brand new."

"I don't care! Throw the darn thing down here."

"All right. When I do, tie it under your arms, and I'll pull you up."

"Okay." The rope dropped sending more dirt rocketing from the side of the old shaft. He could faintly see her shape as she perched precariously on the ledge, gingerly moving to tie the rope around her body without falling off her narrow perch.

"Ready?"

"Yes," she yelled. "Pull me up."

As Dan pulled, she slipped off the ledge and dangled in space. A cry slipped from her lips as she slid into the darkness. Dan braced the sliding rope against his hip, but not before the nylon burned through his fingers. Refusing to release the rope and lose her, he wrapped it around his smarting hands and stopped her fall. A jolt of pain nearly dropped him to his knees as he braced against his injured leg.

With her descent cut off, he pulled against her dead weight. The tension on the rope eased when he heard the crunch of her boots against the side as she pushed against the shaft wall. When her feet slipped, the rope jerked against him. His heart lurched each time he felt her slide back down. Her head slowly came level with the edge of her prison.

"Hold on. Let me secure this end, then I'll get you out of there."

He quickly tied the rope to a tree and hobbled back to the side of the shaft. Dropping to the ground, he reached out and clasped hands with her. He swore softly when the sweat from her palms moistened the raw burns on his fingers. Dan drew her up and out of the hole and across his body as they both rolled back from the edge. They sat up and he looked into her eyes, raised a hand and touched her cheek.

"AJ. . . Damn you scared me."

"I'm sorry. Thanks for getting me out of there, Dan. I thought I was a goner when I saw her right behind me like that. That old mine goes down forever." She stopped suddenly and looked at him. "I'm rambling aren't I?"

"Yeah. I'd say so." He grinned at her. "I'm just glad you're okay."

He shifted and cried out in pain as he tweaked his knee.

AJ was instantly on her feet yanking the rope from her waist to throw it down. "Look at your leg! You shouldn't have been moving on it without the support of the wraps."

"*Me*! Get down here!" Dan grabbed her hand and jerked her down in front of him. "Don't you ever do anything like that again! I thought that stupid moose was going to trample you, then when you fell, I thought it was all over." He grabbed her shoulders and pulled her close. "You scared me half to death."

A tremor shafted through his body as he frowned into her face, moisture gathering in his eyes when his gaze locked with hers. Anger, fear, and concern for her safety warred with each other in Dan's heart. And something else, something undefined. Desire? Love?

Dan suddenly released her. To keep his hands off her, he ran agitated fingers through his unruly hair, the unconscious move bringing more swear words to his lips when his hair caught in the torn flesh of his palms.

A new feeling hit him. He didn't want to leave her. Time, he wanted time to get to know her. Sadness followed the thought. He had to go back to Chicago and to his father's business.

He sighed as he set his hands down in his lap and looked into her eyes again. "Look, I'm sorry, but I don't want you taking chances like that on my account." His look softened as he gave her a cockeyed grin. "Besides, don't I even get a thanks?"

"I told you thanks."

"How about a thank you kiss?"

She drew a deep breath as her spirits soared. Perhaps, just perhaps, he really cared for her. "Of course. Thank you, Dan." She leaned over and gave him a slow kiss. His lips were moist and tasted slightly of the wintergreen he enjoyed.

She pulled back and smiled at him. "What happens to you if you run out of those wintergreens before we get out of here? Will you go through withdrawal?"

"I'll just have to develop a new favorite flavor." He pulled her face close again and kissed her gently, testing, tasting her lips.

The scent of his smooth skin drew her face to his as she softly laid her cheek along his, her hand slipping up his other cheek to slide into his thick hair.

What would it be like to make love to him? To feel his skin against mine?

With a wistful sigh, she sat back on her heels to look at him. Instead of longing, she looked at him with mischief as humor took over anticipation and AJ started to laugh.

"What's so funny?"

"You. I got dirt all over your face. Come on let's go check

out this cabin, and then I'll get our stuff so we can get cleaned up. We need to take care of those burns on your hands." She gazed through the canopy toward a rapidly setting sun. "I think we've gone far enough today."

"I'll buy that. Help me up."

When they were on their feet, AJ pulled his arm around her shoulders and looped hers under his arm and around his waist. Their bodies pressed together as he leaned on her and hobbled along on his good leg. As the nearness of his body caused a tremor to slide through her body, her heart whispered to her. "Take what you can," it said. "Don't miss out on today because you're afraid of tomorrow."

She wanted to listen to the whispers of her heart, but her reason said no. No summer flings. No short term, fly-by-night romances.

As her inner voice and that of her conscience argued, she and Dan moved down the faint trail to the cabin. As the door swung open and AJ helped him through, she wondered at the wisdom of staying overnight in a cozy little cabin with this man.

It was no more than a one-room shack. They stopped in the doorway and simultaneously swung their gazes around the room— a tidy, spotless room. Although small and utilitarian, it had a homey quality. The windows had empty flour sacks for curtains and homemade furniture provided sparse decoration. A small table, single chair and narrow cot were all that occupied the one room structure.

At one side of the cabin was a rock fireplace and hand hewn pine mantel. In front of the hearth was the only store-bought piece of furniture—an oak rocking chair. A small frame on the mantel contained a picture of an elderly man and woman. Next to it stood a photograph of a beautiful college age woman. Both photos were yellowed with age, but not a speck of dust sat on either frame. This was no long-abandoned line shack as AJ had thought.

Dan whispered as though they had entered an unoccupied shrine. "Should we be in here, AJ? It looks like someone lives here."

His question broke her surprised trance, and she helped him across the room and into the old rocker that sat by the river-rock fireplace.

"Sure. What are you whisperin' for?" She looked at him like he was slightly addled. "It's customary up here to leave your place open for travelers caught in trouble. We'll leave a
note and some money to cover what we use."

"This place looks like whoever owns it was just here. Do you think someone could be around?"

"I don't know."

She glanced around the cabin again, and then walked to the kitchen area. Picking up a shiny silver bucket she headed for the door. "You rest while I look around and bring in some water, so we can clean up."

AJ looked at the small stone flower beds around the edges of the log structure. Not a single weed grew between the blooms of orange and gold flowers. A narrow but well-worn path led from the side of the shack to a small shed a hundred feet from the house.

"Hello? Anybody here?" she called out.

Moving along the trail, she listened for a return call from the woods. Perhaps whoever owned the place was out fishing or hunting. When she got no response, she gently opened the door to the tool shed.

"Anybody in here?"

Silence met her as she pushed the door open and stepped into the dim room. A small window with the shutters propped open let a narrow strip of light fall across a work bench. The smell of potting soil, fertilizer, and pesticides met her at the door. Packets of seeds for fairly sophisticated, short-growing-season species were stacked on the bench. Work shelves were stacked with neat rows of gardening supplies.

Puzzled by the state of the shed and house, and the fact that no one seemed to be around, she stepped back out into the afternoon sunlight. A small garden lay at the side of the shed. It was well-placed near a bubbling stream and under a break in the pine canopy to allow the sunlight to reach the plants as much as possible during the short northern summers. Hoping to find some remains of vegetables for dinner, she found the garden meticulously harvested. *Darn, looks like we're back to moss soup for dinner*.

Something about this garden conjured up a childhood memory. The memory of another time and another place. Her grandmother's Victorian house came to mind. As a child she had watched her mother's mother, a silver-haired Swede, canned fresh home-grown produce from her garden. Suddenly she realized what it was about this garden that reminded her of her grandparent's. Turning on her heel she hurried to the creek, filled the pail, and went into the cabin.

"What's up?" Dan asked as she burst through the door.

"I'm not sure yet." She set the full pail on the short rough-wood counter and stooped to pull aside the curtains that hid shelves of pans and dishes. Dropping the fabric she looked into the rafters. There, stored out of the way, was a large kettle and the supplies necessary for canning food.

"Somebody lives in this place year round. Either we just missed him," she shrugged, "or he's hiding from us for some reason."

"What the devil are you jabbering about, AJ?"

"Look up, Dan!"

He did but turned a puzzled gaze on her and lifted his shoulders in a "so what" shrug. "You lost me. It's just some cooking stuff, isn't it?"

"You could say that. I should have known a city slicker like you wouldn't get the implication. Think about it!" With an impatient sound, she gazed at his confused expression.

"Where's the reasoning power you must use everyday at work? I take it no one in your family ever gardened?"

"The gardener grew flowers on the roof patio and kept a few shrubs in good shape, if that's what you mean."

AJ couldn't help it. She laughed at him. "No, that's not what I mean. This stuff isn't just for cooking, it's for canning. Somebody has grown an extensive garden here and put up the food. They wouldn't go to that trouble if they only used this place seasonally. There wasn't a vegetable left in that garden."

"So..."

"If the garden had been used just for fresh food, something would have been left behind because one person could not have eaten everything that garden would produce. Whoever cleaned out the garden took *everything*."

"And...?" he added as though pulling the story from her one clue at a time.

"If I don't miss my guess, I'm going to go back out and find a root cellar dug into the ground pretty close by or burrowed down under the cabin. That means fresh food for dinner! I'll be right back."

Dan looked up a short time later as she returned wearing the smile of a child who found the forbidden cookie jar. She was laden with jars of canned elk, potatoes, green beans, strawberries, and rhubarb.

"That's a lot of food. You sure we won't make the owner come up short."

AJ laughed. "Not hardly. That cellar is loaded!"

"Are you sure that stuff's safe to eat?"

"Of course. Don't tell me you never had home-canned food before either." She looked at him as though he'd been deprived of the basics of life.

Dan grumbled at her. "It's difficult to grow a garden in a penthouse apartment in Chicago. Country living is considerably different than living in the city."

His comment struck a physical blow to her midsection. She knew the lifestyles were different, too different for them to be happy together. Country and city people stayed mixed as successfully as oil and vinegar. Her levity fled as she looked at him.

"Didn't you ever have a house with a yard, even? Surely your parents must have had a place in the suburbs or something."

She grasped at any experiences he might have had that were remotely similar to the life she led as a child. The life she fully intended to continue and knew she couldn't live without. The life she wanted to raise her children in.

"My parents divorced when I was a kid. I lived with my father. We lived in Chicago to be near the business. He didn't see any reason to change that after my mother left. I'll tell you about it sometime." He pointed to the jars in her arms. "What have you got there?"

Realizing he wasn't in the mood to talk about his early years or his family life, she set the food down and told him about her find as proud as an archaeologist with a two thousand year old pot. When she finished showing him, she pointed to the water.

"Why don't you clean up first, then I will. While you do that and rest your leg, I'll get some supper cooking."

As she reached for a metal bowl, she saw him stand and start to unbutton his shirt. The image of his nude and tanned body sprang up before her, the picture as life-like as the hologram of a naked gladiator. A hot stabbing sensation slammed through her body.

AJ turned her back and tried to ignore him. The sound of his shirt pulling free of his pants brought her chin up. She saw his reflection rippling in the warped glass of the small window above the sink where she worked on dinner. His shirt hung open, freed from the waistband where the ends of his belt dangled. The snap on his pants was undone, the zipper part way down. Dan jumped when she dropped the metal container on the counter. He looked at her, one eyebrow raised in a questioning arch.

"I'll...I'll be outside."

A warm knowing smile spread across Dan's face. Her face flushed, AJ hurried out the door letting it bang shut behind her.

Late that afternoon the fragrance of a freshly baked strawberry-rhubarb pie filled the cabin and mingled with that of elk stew. Dan offered to help, but AJ insisted there was little to do thanks to the way the food had been prepared for canning. Instead, he rocked by the fire and watched her at the table, mixing and rolling pie dough. Watched her wipe flour across her freshly washed cheeks with the back of her hand. Watched the ease with which she put together a delicious meal from canned food. She was as at home here as she was in the cockpit of a plane.

After they ate and cleaned up the kitchen, AJ piled more logs on the fire, then sat on the end of the cot. Dan sat in the oak rocker slowly moving back and forth beside her. Outside there was a decided chill in the air. When she had gone out to the privy after supper, a blanket of clouds hid the stars. She had hoped the afternoon wind would blow the storm front over, but the breeze had died down shortly after dinner. Now the clouds were stacking up, billowing higher above the trees, and promising heavy precipitation. In spite of the bone-chilling feel of the air, she prayed it was rain and not snow.

The silence in the room grew strained as AJ and Dan watched the flames dance on the hearth. The closeness of Dan's body to hers was sending heat up and down her spine as surely as if he stroked her body with warm fingertips.

When he shifted uncomfortably, AJ glanced at him then quickly looked back into the fire. Tension bounced around the confining cabin like a shattered atom.

"AJ?"

"Yes?"

"What do you make of this place? It's obvious it's intended for the use of one person. One chair, one small cot. It's been used recently and, as you pointed out, probably year round. Do you think it belongs to a miner or trapper or what?"

"To tell you the truth," she said, "I don't really know what to think. There's no mining equipment in the shed or trapping stuff. He did have that rope you found. That old mine shaft I fell in is the only one I could find around here. It obviously isn't being worked." She paused and thought about his question. "I've seen hermit's cabins before, but they usually aren't this clean and tidy. This place kind of gives me the creeps. As soon as it's daylight, I think we'll be on our way."

"Suits me." A pregnant pause filled the room as he glanced around. The obvious turn of his thoughts brought a mischievous smile to his face. "Any suggestions on who sleeps where?"

AJ had been avoiding that issue all evening. Every time she looked at the small single cot, she envisioned their bodies, naked and entwined under the rough woolen blankets. She seemed to have acquired a vivid imagination that had gone crazy since Dan Satterfield came into her life. What was worse was the power it had to start wave after powerful wave of sensation rolling through her body like whitecaps across Lake Erie in a northeaster.

The heat rose in her face, and she silently regretted her complexion and a face that could be read by any two-year-old.

"You take the cot. With your leg, you need as good a rest as possible. I'll pile a couple blankets on the floor and sleep in my sleeping bag by the fire."

"I can take the floor—or we could share the cot." He smiled suggestively.

"No!" AJ answered too quickly and jumped up, bringing a crooked smile to his face. "No, thanks. You go on and get ready for bed while I make one last trip to the outhouse. I'll be back in a few minutes." As she spoke, she backed away from him. When she reached the door, she grabbed her coat from a hook beside it, then ducked outside.

On the small porch, she gasped for air as though she had just run for her life from a grizzly. Leaning against the post that held up the overhang, she set her forehead against the cold wood and groaned. The hands she wrapped around the pole for support trembled slightly.

What am I doing? He's a city man, a dude. Why am I even thinking about a guy like that?

She shook her head trying to clear the webs that seemed to be wrapping her brain in a fiber cocoon preventing all logical thought. Try as she might, she couldn't keep his image from returning. Disgusted, she decided she was turning into a lusty teenager with the IQ of a turnip. She couldn't stop herself from wondering about him. *He vacations in the wilderness. At least he isn't the kind to be in a Hilton Hotel on an overcrowded beach someplace.*

Her heart started its whispers again, but AJ fought the little voice it seemed to have found on this trip. Pulling her light weight jacket closed against the chill night air, she gazed through the treetops praying for a clear sky and a look at the stars. Instead, she was met with large soft flakes of snow. The size of quarters, they seemed to materialize out of nowhere, free falling from the sky. They drifted down like feathers on a summer breeze, their origin well above her head, lost in the clouds. One landed on her cheek and melted.

She groaned and dropped her chin onto her chest, shaking her head slowly and cursing the timing of the storm as the heavens opened and began dumping snow as though a Hollywood blizzard-making machine had suddenly been turned on.

AJ knew that if this kept up the snow would quickly mount

up, and they would indeed be stranded together in the tiny house for several days. She could only hope that the early storm would be short and the returning fall warmth would quickly melt the snow.

For more than one reason, they had to continue south before something happened she would regret for the rest of her life.

CHAPTER SEVEN

AJ moaned as she stretched, trying to ease the stiffness in her back. All of her joints hurt from sleeping on the floor. She'd take a bed of pine needles over hardwood any day. At least she could level that. The hardwood where she lay was slightly warped slanting toward the hearth. She had spent the night with the uncomfortable feeling that she would be rolling over and over all night.

A dull gray light fell across her face where she lay wrapped in her sleeping bag on the thin blankets she'd put down for padding. She fought to drag herself awake. The night had been a restless one with Dan's image dancing in her dreams. AJ spent the night running from his outstretched arms fearing that if she gave in to his warm embrace, she would be lost.

When her eyes fluttered open she groaned softly. It was still semi-dark outside. She hoped that meant it was early. Reaching for her watch she was forced to acknowledge that it wasn't. The sun should be glaring through the windows. Instead storm clouds rolled around outside. Dark and heavy with moisture, they kept the sun hidden and carried the promise of much more snow to come.

Dan still slept soundly on the small cot. As she watched, a warmth spread over her. His chest rose and fell softly. Chestnut waves tumbled across his forehead. The blankets slipped down revealing bare shoulders. Shoulders that were broad and strong. From the smoothness of his hands, she doubted the muscle came from hard work. Probably belongs to an exec's health club, she thought. Whether he was developed from hard work or workouts didn't matter. The sight of his body, even a small part of it, had her heart skipping like a stone across smooth water. She'd never felt this way about anyone before, especially a virtual stranger.

Why does looking at him give me such a jump-start? The same kind of adrenaline rush she got doing snap rolls in her plane coursed through her as she speculated on seeing more of Dan Satterfield. She had enjoyed their conversation in the plane and although learning little about his personal life, she had enjoyed their discussions of world issues as she attempted to keep his mind off the pain in his leg while they walked.

And his body. Now that was another thing. Every time she looked at him an intense longing and feeling of anticipation rippled through her. Even though it would be an exciting exploration of a fresh and unknown union, she knew she would be as comfortable with him as if she had made love with him a thousand times before. AJ wanted to get close to him. Really close.

Irritated with herself and their situation, she focused her thoughts on the day ahead. What was the best thing for them to do? It didn't include spending the day locked in each other's embrace no matter how badly she wanted it.

Quietly, AJ pushed back the covers and pulled on her boots. Tiptoeing across to the door, she pulled on her jacket and stepped out into a scene that could have been carved from ice crystals. Cold crisp air met her at the door. A pristine coating surrounded her.

In the flower bed at her feet, the gold and reddish brown flower petals barely showed through snow that weighed them

down. The enjoyment of being in a new white world slipped away
quickly when she remembered what it would mean to their leaving
the cabin and heading south. The clouds were threatening to dump
more than the twelve inches she estimated were already down.
Already, tiny specks of snow were spitting at her. They were going
to have to layover, like it or not.

AJ started to step off the stoop and looked down to watch
her footing on the slick surface. She stopped suddenly, a trickle
of fear winding its way up her spine. Boot tracks surrounded the
porch, yet she was positive Dan had not been out all night.
Crunching through the snow, she followed the tracks as they went
from the front steps to the windows of the little house. Someone
had been watching them during the storm, but who? And why
hadn't he made himself known? Especially if this was the owner.

A shiver slid through her body and the hair on her neck stood
like hackles on a dog. She felt as though someone was watching
her. Keeping a watchful eye over her shoulder, AJ hurried to the
outhouse and back again.

She burst into the cabin as Dan pulled on his second boot.
Startled by her sudden appearance, he swung his face toward hers.

"What's going on"

"I'm not sure. Did you go out last night?"

"Are you kidding? It would have taken a stick of dynamite to
get me out in that storm." Before he could voice a question, he
realized what had rattled her. "Is someone out there or just tracks?"

"Tracks. Whoever it was looked in the cabin windows and
went to the root cellar for food, then walked off into the woods. I
didn't follow the tracks to see how far he went."

"Good. Let's gather up our stuff and get out of here. He's
probably just an old hermit who wants his house back."

"As much as I'd love to oblige, I don't think that's wise."

"Why not? It seems foolish to stay now that we know he's
around and obviously not thrilled with our presence. We had a

good rest last night and my leg feels better. What's the hold up?"

"You'll see when you go out. There's at least a foot of snow down and the clouds are really stacking up again. I don't mind walking in the snow, but I don't want to be caught in the open in a blizzard. This time of year the storm should pass quickly. It will warm up for several days before we get hit again. We'll stay put until this passes, then head out at the first opportunity."

"What about our friend?" Dan asked.

AJ shrugged. "I guess we can only hope he's harmless and just shy. How 'bout some breakfast?" She moved to the sink with feigned nonchalance.

Dan followed her and took the plates and silverware from her hands to place them on the table. They were using their aluminum backpacking things, because like everything else in the cabin, they had found only one place setting of dishes and silver.

"Who do you think this guy is? It seems pretty bizarre for someone to live this far out without any apparent means of subsistence other than that garden."

"I don't know. I've never met anyone this reclusive or seen a place quite like this in all the years I've been coming up here. We'll worry about it later. Let's make some hot cakes."

"Sounds great."

The hermit was temporarily forgotten as Dan scrounged in a cupboard for a jug of maple syrup while AJ mixed up pancake batter.

After they had eaten and rinsed the dishes, AJ glanced around the small room. "I wonder if there's anything in here that would tell us about the owner of this place." She stood up and started pacing around the room, looking in cupboards and nooks and crannies for anything that might give them a clue.

"Do you really think you should be snooping around?"

"I'm not just being nosy. I want to know if we have anything to fear from this guy. Don't you think it's a good idea to know what we're up against?"

"I was just asking, go right ahead. Snoop to your heart's content."

AJ sent him a dirty look and stooped down to look under the bed. "Aha!" She pulled a small trunk out from under the springs.

"This has gone far enough. I really don't think we should be looking at someone else's property."

"Don't be such a stuffed shirt. I just want to know who's hiding from us and why. Maybe he's dangerous—a killer or a thief." Her imagination kicked into overdrive as she scooted the chest out of its hiding place.

"Right." Dan's skeptical tone had her sending him an antagonized look that seemed to bounce off his tough hide.

AJ plunked down in the middle of the floor and slowly opened the chest. She gave a disgusted snort as her gaze fell on a relatively new Wall Street Journal. Underneath were several more. Two per year—for the past twenty years.

"I think what we have here is an old stock broker who popped his cork from the stress and ran off to hide from society. Look at these. He must have gotten one each time he went out for supplies." She handed a stack to Dan, then burrowed deeper in the chest. An aging newspaper was almost at the bottom. Yellowed with age, it was starting to crumble around the edges.

Gingerly she pulled it out and held it up to look at the front page. When she unfolded it to read the headlines, the paper cracked and chipped dropping yellowed pieces in her lap. It was dated August 25, 1971.

"Wow!" She let out a slow whistle. "Do you recognize the name James Stone?"

"It sounds familiar, but I couldn't say why. What's that?"

AJ looked up from the paper in her clenched hands. "This says a man by that name was indicted for insider trading and fraud. He posted bail and then skipped out with two million dollars."

"Let me see that." He reached across the trunk that sat between them and took the yellowed paper from her hands.

Dan scanned the article. "I wonder if that's the guy that lives up here. Why on earth would he still be hiding out? I'd have that money and be in Argentina or someplace, not stuck in the wilderness unable to use any of it."

"It would make sense of why he's hiding from us. He might be deranged if he came here from the noise and hustle of Wall Street twenty years ago and never left except for supplies. Even people who have been born and raised up here get cabin fever sometimes."

"Sure. What's that got to do with this?"

"Native Americans who lived in sub-arctic and arctic cultures sometimes went crazy from the severity of the weather and seclusion. They would run off from their villages in a murderous fit of rage."

"What's that got to do with anything?"

"I'm just saying that if they could do it after being born and raised in this country, imagine what the winters and isolation could do to a stock broker from New York City who was virtually trapped up here."

"Point taken." He hesitated. "Well, what do you say now? It seems prudent to me to get out of here. What do you think? Do we stay or go?"

She thought a minute and jumped up from the floor to go to the window. Ominous gray clouds laden with snow swirled outside. A chill wind had come up dropping the temperature and wind chill drastically. The snow already on the ground was being whipped into deep drifts. Clouds raced back and forth ahead of a strong breeze, colliding with one another then billowing higher. AJ knew from experience they were in for more bad weather. Perhaps a storm that would produce a white out that would wipe out their visibility and get them into big trouble if they were in the open.

Turning from the window, she faced him squarely. "We stay. I don't want to get caught in the open when this storm cuts loose. We'll wait for this to pass, and as soon as it's clear, we'll head out."

Dan thought it over and then nodded his agreement.

"Okay. He probably won't bother us anyhow. He would have already if he'd wanted to. He's had plenty of chances. If he thinks we know who he is, he may be in the next county by now."

AJ got down to dig to the bottom of the trunk and gasped when she pulled a small woolen blanket aside. "I don't think so, Dan."

"What?"

"I don't think he's in the next county. I'd say there's a great deal of money in the bottom of this trunk."

Dan bent over her shoulder and looked in. "Whoa! That settles that. We stick together until we can get out of here. Cover that back up and stuff it under the bed. If he shows up we can play dumb about all this."

"We can't just sit here and leave them up there in a blizzard. I say we go regardless," Satterfield said.

Turning from the chintz-covered window, Roy looked up at the determined man standing beside his chair. "Geoffrey, I understand how frustrated you are, but we can't take off in this weather. We wouldn't have any visibility, and it won't help if we go down, too."

"We can't just sit here."

"AJ knows how to survive in weather like this even if they can't find a cabin and are out in the forest. She can build a great little shelter from brush and birch bark in thirty minutes, and you'd be surprised how warm and cozy they can be. Just as soon as the storm lifts, we'll take off."

An deep sigh came from the straight-backed man staring into a crackling fire. "I feel helpless, Roy. We have to do something."

"You have to trust that I know best. Think about it. I couldn't begin to tell you what's best in your business. I know what to do here. Trust me, Geoffrey. We'll find them. I promise you." The promise was made as much to himself as it was to Satterfield Senior.

"You don't understand, Roy. I ...I have to find him and talk to him. There are some things we need to straighten out. I can't lose him before we do that." A slight quiver slipped into the smooth voice as he finished.

Amazed by the show of vulnerability from the rigid autocrat standing at the living room bar, Roy shrugged. "I don't know what your personal reasons are other than you're scared silly, just like me," he added when the other man started to deny it. "I told you we'll find them, and I mean it."

Swinging his chair back, Roy looked helplessly at the heavy snow falling outside obscuring the landing field. *Dear God, why today? Why couldn't you have held off just a few more days?*

Roy glanced at Charlie and saw the concern etched on his friend's face. The man's fear came close to matching Roy's. AJ had been like a surrogate daughter to Charlie. He had never married, never had children of his own. Roy often accused him of being married to the sky.

"Everything will work out, Charlie."

"I know. Soon as this storm breaks up, Ben and I'll have the plane ready to go." Charlie rested his hand on his friend's chair and together they watched the snow swirl around the hotel windows each appearing to pray in his own way for a break in the weather.

***

Lunch finished, AJ stood at the counter rinsing their dishes in a shallow pan. She had carried a pail of snow in and melted it by the fire for dishwater. The delicious smell of fresh bread still lingered in the air. To keep from going stir crazy, she had baked all morning. Although she had never used a small bread oven beside a fireplace, she quickly got the hang of this one.

Absorbed in what she was doing, she didn't realize Dan had come up behind her until he rested his hands on her shoulders. His thumbs slid up the soft skin of her neck as he buried his face in her hair, taking in her scent. AJ moved away from the contact, then tried to ignore it to finish what she was doing. Her hands trembled beneath the surface of the dishwater. Thankful that he couldn't see them, she tried to slow the rise and fall of her breasts as her breath came in short gasps.

"What are you up to, Dan?" Her voice broke. The sound trapped in her suddenly dry throat.

"I'm sorry. I just couldn't resist. You look so domestic doing this. It's like we're man and wife. Here in this cabin, so far from anyone. We could be newlyweds." His head dipped to nibble at her neck as his hands slid up and down her upper arms then back to knead shoulders that had become stiff with his initial contact.

"We could be, but we aren't. You have to be married to be a newlywed, and I haven't played make believe since I was a little girl. So you can just stop that and go away." AJ tried unsuccessfully to shrug off his hands—tried halfheartedly she admitted to herself.

"We could take care of that when we get back to civilization, Aurora." Dan spoke into her ear quietly caressing her with his voice as he pulled her body against his. As the back of her thighs came up against his rock hard form, she jerked upright as though she had touched an electric fence.

"Stop kidding around. We don't even know each other, and I don't appreciate your taking marriage as a joke."

His lips pressed close to her so that his breath fluttered across her sensitive skin when he spoke.

"You're intelligent, honest, beautiful, and strong. What more do I need to know?"

"Apparently you need to know I'm not the kind to take all this lightly. Now stop it and let me finish."

Unheeded, his lips continued moving across the flesh of her shoulder where he had nuzzled his way under the collar of her shirt. Even as she protested, her head fell back against his chest rolling to the side to allow him access to her throat.

A shiver of delight tripped up her spine.

He stopped what he was doing to whisper to her. "We could start our honeymoon here in this quaint little cabin, lying in front of the fire, sipping some homemade wine. We could make it legal when we're out of here."

She groaned. "It's too soon, Dan. We hardly know each other."

"Some things you know from the first moment. I know I want you."

Her blood was racing through her veins and that darned voice was calling her again—whispering to her from the heart. "Take it. He's honest and kind. No one will ever know."

"But I'll know," she blurted.

Startled, he stopped the path his lips made along her shoulder blade. "What?"

"Oh, nothing. I, ah, I was just arguing with myself. We can't do this, Dan. It isn't right. We can't play house just because we got caught up here. We don't love each other, and I'm not getting married to satisfy a physical urge."

He turned her around, handing her a towel to dry her hands. "Is that what you think? That I'm only killing time? That I don't care anything for you?"

"We don't know anything about each other. It takes time for love to grow. We have a physical attraction to one another—I admit that. But it isn't enough. I want it all, Dan." Her eyes misted over as she thought of her parents. "I want what Mom and Dad had. The whole package—a house with a picket fence, a best friend, love, children. The whole shot." AJ hung her head and refused to look him in the eye.

Dan pulled her into his arms, forced her chin up, and kissed her soundly. The kiss was frustrated and possessive at first, then as she responded reluctantly, his lips teased hers apart and became gentle, coaxing. She fell toward him pressing her body against the male length of his. They tasted each other, their tongues joining in age-old rituals as she gave in to the sensations his touch created. Her breasts were full and tingly; her stomach tied in knots. As he moved his lips from hers to travel down the open vee of her shirt, her eyes opened and sought the top of his chestnut hair as she sank her fingers into the masses of waves. She bent her head down and gently kissed the top of his head as he nuzzled between the curves of her breasts. She tasted the slight saltiness of his skin while the fragrance of spicy soap drifted up from his hair.

His lips found the swell of her breast as his hands slid from her back to her ribs and up to cup the underside of her breasts. Dan slipped his hand to the top buttons of her shirt. When he did she shrieked, and he jumped back holding her away from his body so he could look into her face.

"What's the matter?" He could clearly see the terror on her face and realized instantly it wasn't because of him. She was staring out the window.

"He was there. A man was there—watching us."

Dan set her away from him. "Stay here," he ordered. Slowly opening the door, he cautiously stuck his head outside. Whoever it had been was gone, but there were fresh boot tracks under the window. At the edge of the clearing a pine bough swung back and forth shaking heavy clumps of snow from its branches. He banged the door shut and moved a chair over to wedge against it.

"There, that should hold. It's getting a little lighter outside. Maybe the storm will go over tonight, and we can head out in the morning." Looking at her blanched face he asked, "Are you all right, Aurora?"

Unable to speak she simply nodded her head as she rebuttoned her blouse with shaking fingers. She didn't know what had upset her more, the man peeping in the window or the fact that had he not startled her, she would have given herself to this man completely, unequivocally.

With a frustrated sigh, Dan stepped toward her. "Aurora?"

"No! No, Dan. Leave me alone." She quickly turned her back on him and wrapped her arms protectively across her still sensitive breasts.

"How about some coffee? I could use something strong and hot. Stoke up the fire while I start a fresh pot. It's going to be a long afternoon." And night, she thought. A very long night.

CHAPTER EIGHT

Crystalline snow covered the ground. The landscape was turned light as day by an almost full moon. Pine boughs sagged under the weight of new snow heavy with the moisture that comes in a warm early winter storm.

The small dark shape of a man could be seen between the trees surrounding the cabin. The flare of a match stood out against the dark shadow, briefly reflecting the lean bearded features as he lit a cigarette. The match dropped in the snow as he stared at the cabin. Occasionally, the tip of the cigarette glowed red as he drew on it, pulling smoke into his lungs.

He watched the curl of smoke rising slowly from the rock chimney, saw the flicker of flames dancing on the walls of his home through the small glass-paned windows. He had hoped he would never be found. That's why he'd hidden here for so many years. All that work, all of his planning, and he'd barely spent any of the money he'd stolen so long ago.

He was tired of hiding, tired of taking care of people who came looking for him. These two intruders would have to join the others in the bottom of his old mine shaft. He didn't enjoy killing the people who came after him, but he wouldn't give up. Not after all this time. Didn't they understand he was as much a prisoner here as in any prison? *Why can't they leave me alone?*

Tired of letting these strangers take over his home while he slept out in the freezing night, he pulled his collar closer to his neck and threw the burning cigarette down with a disgusted grunt. Turning on his heel, he made his way back into the forest. He had to think about the best way to deal with them. Usually he only had one to worry about.

AJ walked over and gingerly sat on the edge of the cot only to bounce up again and go back to the sink looking for anything to do that would keep her hands and mind occupied. She tried to blame the urge on her upbringing. Her grandmother had always told her the "Idle hands are the Devil's workshop" message of her generation.

Dan rocked in front of the fire. It wasn't a slow peaceful rock, not a quiet relaxing rock, but an agitated keep-moving-at-all-costs rock.

She glanced toward Dan and brought on an instantaneous jack hammering of her heart. AJ realized his presence was as much the cause of her restlessness as her conscience. Unable to find anything else to do, she walked back over and sat down again.

Her gaze slid to his and caught for only a second before she looked away. She opened her mouth to speak, but closed it again, unable to think of anything safe to talk about beyond the weather.

Dan rocked, and rocked. Rocked in quick short arcs. AJ fidgeted, plucking at the plaid woolen blanket on the small cot. Dan cleared his throat, obviously uncomfortable in the continuing silence. Tension crackled in the little room. Tension that was as audible as the snap of the flames on the hearth. They both felt the electricity ricocheting about the room.

AJ jumped when he broke the silence.

"Do you think we can get out of here tomorrow?"

"I don't know. I hope so." *Boy, do I hope so.* "It will depend on how clear it is in the morning. We need the sun to start melting off some of this snow."

"How much farther do you think it is to the river?"

"I looked at the maps earlier, and I'd say we have about twenty miles left. You never know how soon we'll be hit by another storm, either. The sooner we get out of here the
better."

The talk stopped and a palpable silence grew. The silence took on a life of its own, pulsing between them and reminding AJ of house walls just before a tornado bowing out from the pressure and preparing to explode.

Absorbed in her own thoughts, AJ jumped when Dan spoke.

"Tell me about yourself, Aurora. We've skirted all around your family. Tell me about your Indian heritage."

The sound of his voice jolted her. Something in the coaxing quality of it had her blood flowing faster, a soft flush warming her smooth cheeks. AJ stalled trying to think of a way to keep the conversation from turning personal. "You wouldn't find that interesting, Dan. Let's just enjoy the fire."

"Why are you afraid of me? I'm just asking to know more about you. You're always trying to keep things on a business level."

She couldn't argue with a statement that was true, so she didn't try. Deciding that any talk was probably better than the heavy silence of a few minutes before, she sighed and gave in. She shot him a short aggravated look. Dan was the most determined man she had ever had the misfortune to run into.

"There isn't a lot to tell." She nervously slid the tip of her tongue around her lips to moisten their dryness. "My grandparents were Canadian," she began reluctantly. "Gramps was half Chipewyan and half Scottish. My grandmother was all Scot. They lived well north of here near the Barren Grounds. The, ah, tundra area where the Chipewyans made their home."

"Must have been pretty rough living."

"That's right. They still lived as they had for centuries, hunting caribou and using that for the mainstay of their subsistence." Warming to the subject in spite of her earlier reluctance, she explained, "They used the caribou for everything. Meat of course, but also the hides were used for clothes, canoes, and housing. They didn't waste anything. The intestines were even used for making pemmican, a food they could take along with them on hunting expeditions."

"That's disgusting," he said with a frown.

"May be, but it's true. It's really not bad when you get used to it. Anyway, it wasn't easy in the early twentieth century to survive up there. It took hard work and determination to make it through the winter. The promise of an easier life took a lot of the young people south."

"Is that why most of your people headed south?"

"That, and my grandfather was a bit of a rebel. At the time my Gramps was growing up, it wasn't accepted to admit to being part Indian. He kind of rebelled against the Indian ways and wanted to head down into a city, any city, to get away from the Chipewyan nation and to find what he considered a regular job."

"How'd he get into flying?" AJ felt the tension flow out of the room as their discussion turned to family. As it left the cabin, so too it left her body. As usual, the thought of flying and her family brought a tender smile to her lips.

"He saw a stunt flyer who was traveling around barnstorming in the early '30s. He had a dollar in his pocket and hired the man to take him up for a five-minute ride. He was hooked from the first moment the plane left the ground. Gramps went to work for the flyer in exchange for flying lessons and a small salary. Before too long he had saved enough to put a little down on a plane, so he could start a small guide business like ours."

"Is he the one who taught you to do stunts?"

She nodded as her face split with a grin when she thought about those early lessons.

"Gramps had an old Buckerjungmeister." She chuckled at Dan's raised eyebrow. "It was an old biplane, a two seater. He taught me how to fly and how to do stunts in that plane. We had some wonderful times." She grew quiet as she looked into the licking flames, seeing again her grandfather's plane looping across the sky and dancing among the billowing white clouds.

"Did he teach your dad about the survival techniques and Indian ways?"

"No. Like I said, Gramps was a rebel." She shook her head. "He wasn't proud of his background until he was quite old, and I think he got that back because of Dad. See, Dad got his rebelliousness from Gramps, and he fought against accepting the white traditions just as Gramps had the Indian."

"That must have been hard for your grandfather to accept if he worked at moving toward the white ways."

"Yeah, but Pop was determined to learn what he could before the native culture could be lost, so he went north to stay with our relatives in order to learn the ways of the people. Gramps was pretty mad about it, but Dad was determined. Anyway, when he was about eighteen, he took a plane and flew up to the north-country and stayed for a couple of years."

"Is that where you get the name for your company? Was Sky Dancer what they called him?"

"No." A gentle smile crossed her face. "That's my father's nickname for me."

"You?"

"Sure. I've been doing aerobatics since I was fifteen. He thought it was too dangerous for a girl to do, so I was always sneaking off to do them secretly. One day, he came down to the dock and caught me doing stunts over the lake. At the time he was furious. Swore he'd tan my hide if he caught me at it again."

Dan gave her a teasing grin. "Did he?"

"No." She chuckled softly before she continued. "All the time he was chewing me out, I could see a spark of pride in his eye, so it was hard to take him seriously. Later he said the moves were so smooth and graceful that it had looked like I was dancing." She shrugged slightly as she continued. "He called me Sky Dancer and it stuck."

"Does your dad have an Indian name?"

AJ laughed. "Sure does. Crazy Eagle. The Indians named him when they saw him fly in. You know most of the Indian nations, don't use names the same way we do, Joe or Harry or something. They use names that refer to a trait of the person. They thought he was crazy for trying to fly in the sky with the birds, even though they respected what they saw as his ability to soar with the eagles. So that's the way they knew him."

AJ wondered if she'd see her father again, sit and talk about her grandparents, or see her home filled with pictures of her mother and family.

She fell silent and stared into the blue and red flames of the fire. Her long hair fell freely about her shoulders, the flicker of light reflecting off the blue hues as she leaned down to throw more wood on the blaze. Dan reached out and caught a handful of waves just as her hair drifted dangerously close to the heat.

"Careful." His voice caressed even as his hand stroked her hair. "I'd hate to see anything as lovely as this burned." He wrapped the strands of it around his fingers, gently pulling her away from the hearth toward the base of his rocker, catching her in between his powerful thighs as she dropped to her knees between them.

To keep her balance, she braced her hands on his hips. The heat coursing from his body to hers made her tremble. A heartbeat away from him, her lips yearning to press against the fullness of his, she froze, watching the curve of his mouth as his head lowered to hers, watching until his lips captured hers in a burning caress. Her lips parted as she responded, trying to draw him in. Tried to meld with him. Dan nipped at her lower lip. Pain mixed with pleasure jerked her back from the brink of submission. With regret, AJ pulled back from his lips.

As their eyes met, she realized they were once again balanced on the edge of a dangerous precipice and shook her head.

"Let's focus on getting out of here, Dan. Then we'll see what plays out."

Dan didn't agree. He didn't disagree. He released her hair, setting her free, then sat back in the chair and turned his gaze to the fire that cast shadows about the room and on the walls.

AJ rocked back onto her heels as she sucked in a long quivering breath. It was a futile attempt to slow her racing heart. Pushing up from the floor, she hurried to put some space between their trembling bodies as chaotic sensations tumbled through hers.

"How 'bout some coffee?" She didn't wait for an answer although he grunted one. Taking down the blue and white enamelware pot, AJ filled it with coffee grounds and water and carried it over to the fireplace. Grabbing a potholder, she swung the hook out to hang the coffeepot over the fire.

AJ bent over and settled the pot on the metal hook, the fabric of her jeans stretched over her body clinging to her legs and backside. Without warning, Dan reached out and grabbed her, pulling her onto his lap.

She let out a squeal and landed on him. "What the devil do you think you're doing?"

"We're going to talk. I've had enough of this. I feel like this rocker's an ejector seat, and I'm just waiting for the roof to blow off this place for it to send me into orbit."

AJ tried to slide off his lap. He forced her back. "Sit still. We both keep dodging the fact that we're attracted to one another in a big way. I want to know why you're so resistant to it."

She opened her mouth to speak but he cut her off.

"And don't give me the two different worlds story. I don't buy it. You're a pilot and we both own airplanes. I'd say we could commute pretty easily, so something else is going on in that beautiful head of yours. Is there something else about me you don't like or trust?"

AJ looked down on his face. A face that reflected character and integrity. A face that had the annoying habit of drifting in and out of her dreams. His green eyes were the emerald of a deep still sea as he gazed at her. She knew she had to leave quickly or drown in his look.

"Let me go, Dan," she demanded quietly. Leaning forward she pushed away and tried again to get up, but he pulled her back down on his lap and held her fast.

"No you don't. I asked you a question, and I think I deserve an answer."

She hesitated a split second as she considered refusing to answer, but decided that would be childish. "I told you, Dan. I want it all, and I think you're only looking for a quick romance." She looked away from him, afraid to continue looking into those eyes, afraid to watch the firelight casting golden sparks of light through his hair.

Dan's big hand came up to capture her chin.

Insistently he brought her face back to his. "That's a farce and you know it."

"Let me up, Dan."

"All right, but I want some answers. Talk to me, AJ."

Her heart tripped and danced beneath her breast, slamming against her ribs like a pile driver. Her palms grew damp. She nervously ran them up and down her legs to dry them on the denim as she paced in front of him. She could still the heat from his body on the back of her legs, remembered the way he'd reacted to her.

At that moment, she doubted she could speak if her life depended upon it. She had to do something, anything, or things were going to get out of hand very quickly. Dan was looking at her as though he could devour her with his eyes, and she knew she wouldn't resist, couldn't—not for long.

"Aurora?" He spoke her name gently. "Where's your mother?"

A frown tugged at the corners of her mouth. She waited, hoping to compose herself before she answered.

"What makes you ask that? She doesn't have anything to do with us."

"I've been thinking about it, and I think she may have more to do with us than you want to admit. You never mention her. The one time I did, you cut me off. Did something happen with her that prevents you from trusting me? Did someone hurt you, or did they hurt her?"

Her chest tightened forcing the air from her lungs. The pain she felt was as fresh as it ever had been. Her chin trembled slightly as her gaze met his. "No one hurt Mom or me.

It was what happened to my father. I told you Mom...she died."

"I'm know. I'm sorry." He took her hand and rubbed the back of it across his jaw while his other hand ran reassuringly up and down her arm. "Tell me what happened," he said.

It was an order, issued in a quiet voice, but firm enough to let her know he would accept nothing short of the truth. Still she hesitated, not sure she wanted to face the pain she had kept buried. She gave in with a small shrug before her shoulders slumped.

"Four years ago Mom and Dad had a flight to make. They were going north for the wedding of a good friend. Dad had a new red and white, four-seater Fairchild." AJ tugged on the buttons of her shirt. "Mom was worried. She had a sixth sense about those things, and she felt something wasn't right. But the plane was new and the weather good, so Daddy talked her out of her concern and they went anyway."

Dan caught her hand, stopped her pulling against the fabric.

"They were about halfway when a sudden storm came up. It was an early winter storm like this one, and it was quite cold. Ice kept gathering on the wings, but they didn't have anywhere to land. Afraid they couldn't make it back, Dad kept going. He dropped down to find slightly warmer air. Anything to get the ice off the wings..." She fell silent, staring into space.

"And?" Dan prompted.

"Before he could reach a lake to set down on, the ice got too bad. He, ah, he lost control. He did his damnedest to land it in one piece, but couldn't pull it off." AJ stopped to pull in a quaking breath so she could go on. "They weren't as lucky as we were. They careened through the forest and before the plane stopped, they slammed into a huge tree. It hit Mom's side of the plane and killed her outright."

"God, I'm sorry. What about your father?"

"The engine block was forced back into Dad's lap, crushing his legs. His hands and arms were badly cut by flying glass when the windshield shattered. He lay in that plane for forty-eight hours before he was found and given some medical attention. That plane crash crippled him. They said it was a miracle he didn't die of exposure. In the beginning, I think he wished he had..." Her voice trailed off.

She had been staring into the fire, and when he gently turned her face so he could look at her, tears slipped silently down her cheeks. He raised a fingertip and traced their path, wiping the moisture from her face before he pulled her tightly into the protective circle of his arms, forcing her head down onto his chest. As she finally gave in to the pain trapped within her since the wreck, she sobbed quietly, drenching the front of his shirt. He held her murmuring softly against her hair and gently rocking her in the warm oak chair. When her sobs finally stopped, he pulled a handkerchief from his pocket and handed it to her, pulling her chin up. She could easily read pain on his features that matched her own.

"Had you cried at all, Aurora? Or have you been holding this in the whole time?"

She shrugged self-consciously. "Dad needed me. Someone had to be strong." She hiccuped, wiping her runny nose like a child. "He was crushed when he lost her. I wasn't sure if he'd make it or not. At times I thought he'd die of a broken heart. I didn't have time to give in to feeling sorry for myself."

Dan gave a disgusted snort. "It isn't feeling sorry for yourself to grieve when you lose someone so close to you. Women take this nurturing business too far. You've got to learn to take care of yourselves, too. Wasn't there anyone to help you with this?"

Feeling defensive at his tone, AJ hastened to explain. "My brother was already out on his own. I had to take care of my little sister until she left for college. Of course, there's always been Charlie. He was with us through it all."

For a while they rocked, AJ absorbing the comfort of his arms as he silently held her in his arms. Occasionally his hand strayed to the waves that floated down her back, gently stroking them.

"AJ, what does all this have to do with us?"

"I guess I never really thought about it before, because I never had more than a casual interest in anyone." She tried to turn away, but he brought her face close to his, so that she felt his warm breath fanning her face.

"Dan, I'm starting to really care about you and that scares me. I don't want an all consuming love like my father had and to lose that love. I'd rather not love at all than to have it and lose it so suddenly."

"You said before you didn't want a quick romance, now you say you don't want a lifelong love. You can't have it both ways. Make up your mind what you want and go after it. You can't hide away from life, Aurora. That's no life at all. You've got to let go and take life as it comes." Dan shrugged against her.

"This is all happening so fast."

"We have to wait and see what happens. I know it sounds trite, but if you don't live life to the fullest, you'll miss out on it all. I'm not going to let you screw up both our lives if we have something special starting here."

His voice softened as the rocking of the chair slowed, then stopped. Mesmerized, she watched as his hand came up in slow motion to cup the back of her head. With only the slightest pressure, he had her lips sinking down to meet his. The joining was gentle at first, but the desire he had banked for so long sparked and burst into flame at her first tentative touch. Dan's lips took her mouth, starved for the taste of her. His tongue touched and teased. As her lips opened to his, their mouths mated. A groan came from deep within his body as they drew each other in.

AJ's hands sank into his hair as she tried desperately to draw him closer. Gradually she released his mouth and guided his face into the cleft between her breasts hugging him close to her body. With her eyes closed she took a deep breath and tried to maintain some semblance of control. He flicked the tip of his tongue across the flesh of the upper swells of her breasts as his hand came up and impatiently unfastened the buttons of her blouse. Giving up, she laid her head back against his shoulder, exposing her throat to his roving lips.

Eager to be close to her naked body, he pulled her blouse aside and carefully, reverently, freed one of her breasts from the lace cup of her bra. His fingers brushed the curve of it.

Tested the taut peak. When he saw it tighten and deepen in color, his longing for her stole the breath from his body.

"You're beautiful, Aurora. Exquisite," he whispered.

His head lowered slowly, lips gently brushing across her flesh. Short day's-end whiskers scraped her skin sending a shiver of delight through her breasts. When his mouth circled the rosy tip, she cried out as sensation after sensation rolled through her body.

Beneath her she felt him growing again. Eager to feel his body, she slipped her hand inside his shirt, brushing her fingertips across his sinewy chest. When she touched him, a gasp of pleasure escaped from his lips. He raised his head to reclaim her mouth. AJ shifted her weight slightly to run her free hand up and down his inner thigh between their bodies.

When the sound of stomping boots reached them, AJ gasped and swung her gaze toward the front porch. As a pounding began on the door, she was already pulling her blouse closed over her bared breasts, her face flaming hot. Dan swore profusely damning everyone in the country to hell as he set her away from him. He yanked his flannel shirt closed and left the tail hanging out to cover the evidence of his lack of control.

"Just a minute," he shouted. "Hold on, I'm coming."

When he reached the door and started to pull away the chair that had been bracing it shut, he glanced back at AJ to make sure she was covered.

"Who is it?" As he waited for an answer he motioned for her to step back, then bent over the counter and picked up the large frying pan she had used to cook dinner.

Ready to pounce if need be, Dan slowly swung the door open. In the open doorway stood a seemingly harmless, grumbling middle aged man. Snow clung to his coat and hat, large clumps still stubbornly hanging onto his boots. A few large flakes melted on his beard and eyelashes when the warm air of the cabin hit his face. He looked far older than he should have, if he was the thief in the newspaper article she'd found.

"Who do you think it is?" the man snapped. He advanced into the room shaking snow off his small body as he did. "I'm John Smith. This is my house—who the hell are you?"

CHAPTER NINE

White scars stood out against the tan skin of Roy's slightly gnarled hands where they lay in his lifeless lap. Periodically, the fingers that knotted together would unfurl to form a church steeple like the one in the childhood game he had played with AJ. Roy glanced around the Hilton's VIP suite. How ironic that they were trapped in a civilized white world, surrounded by an all white room, in a hotel engulfed in a blizzard of white, while AJ and Dan were trapped in a wilderness turned white with the first evidence of winter.

Satterfield's suite was winter white, from the plush carpet to the furnishings, to the drapes. The only signs of color were the throw pillows on the sofa and the paintings that had been tastefully hung about the room. Linen fabrics of forest green and shades of brown were highlighted by soft peach and pale green shades that graced the oils hanging silently on the walls.

Where are they? Where is AJ spending the night? An unseen fist clutched at Roy's insides, twisting. *Is she still alive?*

"Roy." Geoffrey drew his attention from the blizzard swirling around outside. "Scotch or Bourbon?"

Roy sent him a crooked smile. "Scotch—of course." The smile faded as quickly as it had come. His gaze returned to the whiteout beyond the window.

Satterfield handed him the glass, effectively drawing him out of his reverie.

"Thanks." The sound stuck in his throat where it had tightened around a lump the size of a pine cone at the thought of AJ. He was getting used to the feel of it. It had become a constant companion over the last several days, as had the knots in his stomach.

Roy looked at Geoffrey, trying to assess his new friend's state of mind. The two had been brought together by the possible loss of their children. In the hours since they had met, the fear and devastation each felt drew them close. Common interests besides their children were being discovered and a bond was forming.

Geoffrey spoke in a falsely light tone. "Drink up, Roy. Everything will be fine. Isn't that what you promised me?"

"Right." He forced his sagging shoulders back and plastered a weak smile on his face. "Right! Ben, what's the weather report for tomorrow?"

"Looks pretty good. This storm's supposed to break up and be followed by warmer temps tomorrow. It may cloud up on us again later in the day, but that's supposed to be a fast moving warm front that might only dump a couple of inches of snow before warming up again the day after. We should get several hours of flight time in before that moves in."

"Great. What's the flight plan, then?" Roy asked.

The younger pilot set his glass aside and reached for a map of northern Canada. Before he could answer, a tentative knock slipped across the room from the outer suite door. The men hesitated, at first unsure they had actually heard something. Slightly louder this time, the knock came again.

"Excuse me. I'll see who that is."

As Geoffrey walked softly to the door, his footsteps muffled by the thick carpet, Roy, Charlie, and Ben bent over the map spread across the coffee table. In the foyer the door swung open. A sound of surprise escaped from the man standing rigidly in the opening. The others looked up at Geoffrey's exclamation, glancing toward the scene unfolding in the doorway.

Standing in the hall was one of the most striking women Roy had ever seen. A petite woman with a slim but shapely figure, striking green eyes, and auburn hair. Hair with streaks of silver that she had obviously not felt the need to hide. Roy had the impression she was completely composed and in control, yet a high voltage charge bounced between the two people in the foyer setting off sparks and threatening to ignite an explosion. Standing unobtrusively behind her, a uniformed bellboy held her luggage apparently unclear as to whether he should bring it into the room or not.

Roy believed that if they had not been there to witness it, Geoffrey would have slammed the door in her face.

"What the devil are you doing here, Marjorie?" Geoffrey snapped.

"Aren't you going to ask me in?" Even as she posed the question, she sidestepped him and slipped into the room, motioning for the bellboy to set her luggage inside the door. Opening a black Gucci bag, she slipped the young man a tip as he thanked her and hurried from the suite. Turning into the living room, she glanced at Roy, Ben, and Charlie.

"Gentlemen." She nodded to them.

Charlie and Ben stood to greet her and Roy just gestured toward his wheel chair. "Forgive me, ma'am."

"My husband seems to have forgotten his manners. I'm Marjorie Satterfield." She crossed the room and extended her hand to each man in turn as they introduced themselves.

Roy watched as Geoffrey, with deadly quiet, closed the door behind the rapidly retreating bellboy and moved toward the woman, stalking her like a cobra intent on a kill. His face was a mask of resentment. *Lot's of history here*, Roy thought.

Ignoring the others, Geoffrey glared at her. "It's ex-husband. Why are you here?"

Marjorie flashed an angry glance at him. "My only child is presumably lost in a plane crash. Did you really think I would stay away?"

His jaw tightened as he glared at her. "How did you find out? We've been careful to keep their names out of the news."

Roy watched the interchange, admiring her for her apparent determination.

Standing her ground, she raised her chin slightly. "Jonathan called me. It seems your attorney, at least, understands I have a right to know what is happening to my son."

The air in the room snapped and crackled like the flames of the fire, and as she paused to draw a breath to continue, Roy hurried to break into the conversation.

"Thanks for the drink, Satterfield. Boys, let's get going. We should make this an early night to be in the air first thing. Geoffrey, we'll meet you at the airport at six o'clock. Mrs. Satterfield, it was a pleasure meeting you."

Geoffrey nodded his agreement, but said nothing as Ben quickly rolled up the maps, and Charlie wheeled Roy toward the door. Grabbing their coats, they let themselves out into the hall, thankful to escape.

Geoffrey watched the door swing closed then turned back to the woman in front of him. His hands were clenched in fists and his back ramrod straight.

He watched as she pulled off black kid gloves and the steel gray coat then gracefully lowered herself onto the sofa. As she crossed her exquisitely shaped legs, Geoffrey's gaze slid down the length of them to rest momentarily on her slim ankles. She still had the legs of a dancer. In spite of his anger, he was not unmoved by her seasoned beauty. The emerald green of her light wool dress deepened the shade of her eyes and was the perfect foil for her auburn hair. She had always been able to show off her understated beauty in a classy, tasteful way. He hadn't seen her in over twenty years, but she was more beautiful than ever.

The first shock of seeing her began to wear off. "I believe I could use another drink. Would you like one?" She shook her head, and he moved to the wet bar to fix himself another Scotch. He could feel her watching him, and when he glanced up, their gazes met across the living room. Angry or not, he had to admit she could still make his blood boil. Their marriage had been far from a smooth ride. He had enjoyed their tempestuous relationship. The thought of the energy they had put into their fights, as well as their making up, had a long quiet hunger growing deep in his loins.

Moving back to her, he stopped to stir up the blaze in the fireplace and to throw another log on the coals. Unable to delay any longer, he sank down opposite her in an overstuffed armchair.

He came straight to the point. "Why did you come, Marjorie? You haven't seen fit to care about Daniel before this."

Her face turned the color of old chalk at his calculated statement before she faced him squarely. "That's not true and you know it. I love Dan as much as you, if not more. At least mine is an unselfish love."

"What do you mean by that?"

Impatient, she sprang to her feet and began pacing along the back of the sofa.

"When I left you, I didn't have anything. You had power and money, and the connections to win a custody battle against me. I also knew you could give Dan the best education available and the best possible care. I gave him up so he could continue to be raised with the advantages I never had."

"Did you think money and position were more important than

the love of his mother?" He remembered well the twelve-year-old boy hiding his tears, crying in his room at night when he thought no one would hear.

She sighed and walked to the mahogany bar. Crystal clinked against crystal as she poured sherry from a decanter into a small flute. He saw her hands tremble as she returned to her place on the sofa.

"At the time I thought those things were important. I wanted him to have the best, the best schools, the best chance at a good life. Anyway, after what you did to me, to our marriage, I wasn't going to take one red cent from you. I couldn't have given Dan anything, and I thought that meant something. Now I know better. Besides," she challenged over the lip of the flute, "have you forgotten the agreement you made me sign relinquishing all my parental rights?"

Geoffrey pushed aside the rush of guilt that slashed through him like a scalpel, choosing instead to refocus the blame on her for her separation from their son. "How do you think he felt being deserted by his mother when he was only twelve?"

Looking up from where the amber sherry swirled in the tiny glass in her hands, she looked straight at Geoffrey as though by meeting his direct gaze she could see what he was thinking.

"I know exactly how he felt. When he reached eighteen and graduated from high school, I decided it was well past time for him to know the truth. We've been seeing each other frequently for the last fourteen years."

He couldn't have been more surprised if he had been shot out of a cannon. Her quiet statement brought him to his feet. His voice was deadly as he asked, "You what?"

"You heard me. You never would admit that the divorce was mostly your fault, and Dan felt that you would resent our seeing each other. We both decided it was best not to tell you about our meetings since you seemed so bitter. We've grown quite close actually." She drained the last of her drink, set the glass on the table and stood up. "Which room is the extra one?"

"You're not staying here!"

"Of course I am, and furthermore, I'm going with you in the morning."

"You can't. The plane we brought is a four-seater, and it's full."

"Then talk to Roy and arrange another. I'm going. Now, show me to my room. I want to get some rest. It's been a long day."

Geoffrey shook his head, half in disgust and half in admiration. She still had spunk, and he had to admire her style. That was what he had fallen in love with all those years ago. With a small bow of his head, he raised his arm and held his hand out palm up to point her toward the extra bedroom.

When she closed the door softly behind her, he turned and picked up his drink, moving to stand at the windows, staring into the darkness and wondering what might have been if he hadn't broken her trust and ruined their marriage. It had taken several years and a disastrous second marriage, but he finally accepted his role in the demise of the first. He had carelessly killed a love that he had believed would last a lifetime.

He stared into the falling snow visible around the outside lights of the hotel. His thoughts swirled as rapidly as the blowing flakes while he stood lost in his own memories.

Roy and the others stopped to pick up their room keys at the desk. As he swung away from the receptionist, a small man got into the elevator. Something about the way the man moved struck him as being familiar. As the elevator doors slipped closed, the man turned toward the front, momentarily meeting Roy gaze. There was no doubt that the two men knew each other well. Charlie watched, too.

"What do you suppose he's doing here, Charlie?"

The red-haired Scot shook his head. "I didn't know Jorgensen did business up here. Do you think his being here is just a coincidence?"

"I don't know, but I intend to find out. Let's just keep an eye out for him and see what happens while I do."

A chill wind blew swirling snow across the bare hardwood floor before Dan could force it closed behind John Smith. The man moved across to the fire, pulled his thick gloves off, and began warming his hands as he rubbed them together above the flames.

"That coffee I smell in the pot?"

AJ nodded as he sent a questioning look toward her. "Well, don't just stand there, girl. Get me a cup. I'm 'bout froze to death."

She hurried to the counter and grabbed a tin cup, filled it for the aging man and handed it to him. "Won't you sit, sit down?" she stuttered.

"That's mighty cordial of you, considerin' this is my house."

"Sorry. I, um, wasn't thinking." AJ shrugged and backed a few steps away.

"Mr. Smith, we're sorry about invading your home without your permission," Dan said. "Our plane crashed six days ago, and we're working our way south. We got caught by the snowstorm and had to find shelter. We'll pay you for the provisions we've used."

Small eyes darted looks first at Dan, then at AJ. As the man openly stared at them, AJ got more and more uncomfortable.

"Look, Mr. Smith, we'll be out of here as soon as the storm breaks. There really wasn't anything else we could do."

A smile slipped across the weathered features visible through the light beard. Dirty gray streaks filtered through the dark hair that, though uncombed and untidy, appeared to have been recently cut.

An uneasy silence blanketed the room as the man sipped the hot coffee, and Dan and AJ waited. Waited for the owner of the cabin to finish his drink and have something to say.

Handing the empty cup to her, Smith stood up and reached for his coat. "I'm going out before I turn in for the night. This is my house, and I'm older than you two are—I get the cot. You can share the floor, but when this storm blows over I want you out of my house." Turning, abruptly he slammed out the door, again letting cold air pour in as he crossed the threshold.

Slowly Dan turned to AJ. "What do you think?"

"He gives me the creeps—John Smith. How stupid does he think we are?"

"Remember, he doesn't know we found the trunk. Actually what I meant was, doesn't something about him strike you as odd?"

"Everything! Did you have something in particular in mind?"

"Yeah. Did you notice his hair is unkempt yet it looks freshly cut like he's just been somewhere to get it styled? And that beard, that's not the beard I would expect on a backwoodsman. That's only a couple of days growth."

AJ joined in. "Did you notice the quality of his clothes? They aren't brand new, but they were expensive when they were, and they're in good shape for someone who wants us to think he's nothing but a hermit."

"Aurora, tonight we stick together and first thing tomorrow, snow or not, we're getting out of here. There's no telling how far he'll go to protect his nest egg if he thinks we know who he really is and..."

The sound of stomping boots stopped Dan in mid-sentence. He sent her a reassuring smile as the door blew open chilling the little room with the frigid night air. Large snow flakes swirled around in circles on the floor. Smith put his shoulder to the door and forced it closed against the winter storm.

"AJ, let's take a walk to the outhouse, then we can turn in, too."

She nodded silently and reached for her jacket, then led the way outside. When they returned Smith was in bed, breathing deeply and snoring softly, presumably already sleeping.

With a shrug, Dan lay down on the bedroll they spread out on the floor, pulling her down, too. With AJ between his body and the cot, Dan lay with his arm protectively around her, facing the cot so he could keep his eye on the weasel-like man on the bed.

AJ stiffened against his chest as he pulled her close. His warm breath fluttered through her hair, and her head rested on his chest. The slow rhythmic beat of his heart pounded against her skin where her cheek pressed against his chest. Erotic sensations plummeted through her body. She'd never be able to sleep in such a position, but she didn't care about that. She never wanted this to stop, never wanted to lose him.

"Dan?"

"Shhh, Aurora. Sleep now. You need your rest. We'll have plenty of time together when we get out of this." His large hand spread across her hair, slowly massaging her back and shoulders beneath it.

Tomorrow is soon enough to worry. Tomorrow. A low moan escaped her as she gave in to the delightful feelings Dan caused to filter from the tips of her long hair to her toes. AJ closed her eyes and let her mind drift into dreams. Dreams of a tall, strong body dressed in denim and wool plaid. Dreams where that man was beside her in the cockpit, dancing among the clouds.

CHAPTER TEN

The pinkish-gray light of dawn filtered through the small window and fell across AJ and Dan where they lay on the hardwood floor. Dan had dozed fitfully as she snuggled close to his body and slept soundly throughout the night.

Coming awake in the growing light, Dan looked over at the still sleeping form of their crotchety host. He appeared to have hardly moved all night. His snoring frame remained burrowed under the worn wool cover where it had been the past ten hours.

The sunlight peeking through the window promised a storm-free day.

Gently, Dan shook AJ's shoulder. "Wake up," he whispered. "I want to get out of here before he wakes up." His lips grazed across her forehead, lingered on her ebony hair where he crushed it to his face to release its scent.

Slowly her eyes fluttered open and she leaned back a little to look into his face, a soft sleepy smile forming on her lips. The smile made Dan wonder what would it be like to awaken this way every day for the rest of his life. His imagination conjured up a vision of AJ's body entwined with his under a down comforter in a large four poster bed. From outside would come the sound of a lake gently lapping at the dock as he made love to her. A sound of pure pleasure slipped from deep in his chest. Dan brought himself up sharp. *We've got to get out of here.*

"Aurora." He shook her shoulder and brought her fully awake. "Come on. Let's gather up our stuff and get out of here." He threw back the edge of the blankets and stood up, pulling her to her feet.

AJ watched as he moved stiffly to gather their things. "How's your leg? Are you going to be able to walk in the snow? It won't take long for most of it to melt when the suns get up more, but it's pretty deep right now."

"We'll make it. I'm just a little sore this morning. It'll work out as we go."

"In your infinite macho wisdom, you wouldn't complain about it if your life depended on it, would you?"

He grinned. "Probably not." He turned her away and gave her a shove toward their gear. "Let's get organized," he said quietly.

They moved around the cabin as carefully as possible, listening for any change in the breathing of the man curled on the cot. The fire had died down during the night and the room was chilly, helping to keep him warmly bundled and oblivious to them on the sagging bed. He slept soundly in spite of their movements.

Smith watched AJ and Dan step off the porch into over a foot of fresh snow, take a quick compass reading and head south. When they left the cabin clearing and faded into the forest, Smith slowly climbed onto the kitchen chair and reached into the rafters for a rolled up blanket. He brought it down and laid it on the table, jumped off the chair, and carefully pulled the blanket aside to reveal a Winchester .30-30.

Reverently he rubbed his hand over the polished wooden stock. The initials JS had been painstakingly carved into the butt of the weapon, as had the delicate roses that had graced his New York gardens. God knew he'd had plenty of empty hours to whittle during the long winter nights. He had gotten quite good at woodcarving. He had even come to accept the quiet and loneliness.

Now they were going to ruin it all if he didn't stop them. With a sigh of resignation he pulled on his coat, picked up the rifle and left the cabin. Confident he could catch them quickly, he didn't bother with gathering any supplies for his outing. Picking up their trail was no problem in the fresh snow, and shouldering the weapon, he set off at a steady pace to make sure they never made it out of the forest.

As the sun topped the two hundred and fifty-year-old pines, Roy and his group winged their way north in a Queen Air twin engine plane. Roy had not questioned Geoffrey's request for a larger plane. Assuming Marjorie Satterfield would be joining them, he had already chartered the eight-seater for the duration of their search when Satterfield had called him at his hotel late the night before.

The search parties moved east from the Ogoki area and were getting closer to the heading AJ was using to get them to the Fort Albany River. Because of the density of the forest canopy, the search planes had been flying narrow north-south transects in an attempt to spot the downed plane through the trees. Every small lake and pond had been checked in the hope AJ had simply set down due to some kind of mechanical difficulty.

Ben brought the plane down as they reached the start of the first search area. As they skimmed the treetops keeping their eyes trained constantly on the ground, Roy spoke to Geoffrey.

"What'd you do about my seeing that guy I told you about at the hotel yesterday?"

"Hmm? Oh, sorry, I thought I mentioned that. I called a man I know in Chicago, and he's running a check on him. He'll let us know as soon as he gets anything."

"Good," Roy said. "He's a thief and a liar. I wouldn't put it past him to have had a hand in this."

AJ stopped her crunching footsteps to listen. Dan had come up behind her. "What...?"

"Shhh! Don't you hear that?"

He listened a moment then shook his head. "Wishful thinking. I don't hear anything. You've stopped us a dozen times, and it's never anything."

"I say it's a plane. I can feel it coming. I can hear it." She started to bounce around looking for a clearing where they could see and be seen. Spotting a small thin spot a short distance away, she dropped her gear in the snow and ran to it gazing skyward. The sound of the twin engines increased slightly then began to move away.

"You said nobody'd be looking for us." A crooked grin curved his lips, put the dimple back in his cheek.

"I know, but I lied." She wiggled her eyebrows making him laugh. "I didn't want you to be complacent enough to want to just sit and wait. They're looking for us, Dan. I knew they would."

He stood beside her, his arm laid over her shoulders. "But, they didn't come this way. How do you know they're looking for us?"

"I just do, okay? They'll be back, and soon they'll be right over us if we stay on this heading. That plane was flying due north, probably flying a search pattern. They may not get to us today, but I tell you they're coming. They have to locate us, then we'll rendezvous at a landing place, and they'll get us."

AJ did a little jig as excitement flowed from her, bringing an indulgent chuckle to Dan's lips. Still watching the sky as though to draw the plane back, she lost her balance in the snow and landed on her backside in a drift.

Laughing, he reached down and hauled her to her feet, turned her around, and brushed the snow from her pants before it melted and soaked in. When he finished, she spun around and launched herself at him. Excited at the prospect of being found and going home soon, she threw her arms around him, pulling his head down, so she could plant a premature celebration kiss on his mouth. When her lips met his, his arms closed around her body to pull her against the sinewy length of his thighs. The lightness of the kiss changed as his lips demanded a greater response from hers.

AJ recognized the power she held over him as his heart thudded against his jacket, close to her own breast. Her lips opened to his, giving and taking at the same time. His tongue darted in and out of her mouth, taunting and placating at once.

She tasted and tempted him as emotions as pagan and wild as the forest rampaged uncontrolled through her body. Dan shuddered against her. Reluctantly, he drew back from her lips. One look at his face let AJ know how much restraint he was exercising at that moment. The instant he reined in his passion, she realized what she wanted him to do to her. She pulled back as far as his gripping hands would allow.

He slid his hands up her arms to her face and slowly gave her one more kiss, a sweet, gentle kiss. He savored the taste of her lips then raised his head and uttered a quivering sigh.

"I would love to keep this up all day, but we've got to keep moving."

"I know," AJ agreed, her voice a husky whisper. "It's just as well. We can't give in to this until we're sure."

Dan's irritation grew. "What aren't you sure about? That care for each other?"

"I'm sorry, Dan. I have to be sure this is the right choice, at least for me. I already told you I don't play house, and I don't take sex casually."

"Is that all you think this is to me—sex?" He made the word sound dirty. "Sex is what a man has with a woman he picks up in a bar for the evening. It's what he has when he and his partner are looking for no more than a physical release. Do you really think that's all I want from you?" he asked, looking into her eyes.

AJ dropped her gaze. "No. I guess not." She hesitated. "I don't know! We barely know each other. How can I tell?"

"There's no time limit on how long it takes to care or to love, Aurora. You have to decide if what you're feeling is lust or love, and only you can decide if you trust me with your heart and your body." He pressed his lips to her temple then turned her away, impatient with himself, with her, with the joke life seemed to be playing on them. His voice was gruff from frustration and disappointment. "Come on, let's get going."

He tried to lighten the moment. "Besides, which snow drift would you like to make love in?"

She followed his lead and chuckled.

"AJ? It'll all work out. Don't worry about it. Right now we have more important things to consider. Why don't you get your gear and we'll move on?"

Not one to feel sorry for herself or to stay in a blue mood, she forced her inner energy into her steps. Gathering up their gear, they headed out once again.

Breaking from the light underbrush, AJ and Dan came to a steep bluff. They followed a deer trail that wound back and forth up the side of it. Slipping on the wet rocks and loose pine duff, AJ fell back and slammed to a stop against Dan.

"Whoa," he said, grabbing her to keep her from falling to the bottom. "Let me go first and see if I can dig in with my stick."

Moving up the slope, he reached back with his free hand and clasped AJ's smaller one in his own. As his hand engulfed hers, she looked into his face. A tremor skated up the length of her spine at the warm contact of his skin on hers. A look of hope leapt to her eyes as she saw his concern for her reflected in his own. He hesitated only a moment before smiling at her and then turning to head uphill again.

He loves you, whispered her heart. *Accept it and run with it. Don't be afraid.*

"Easy for you to say."

Dan stopped and turned back. "What?"

"Sorry. I was, well, talking to myself again."

"I don't know about you," he teased. "Am I safe depending on a woman who talks to herself to get me out of the Canadian wilderness alive?"

She gave him a playful shove, and they started climbing again. They made their way up, sometimes sliding down and having to try another trail. Part way up, a sound drifted to them from behind. AJ stopped and listened. The forest was silent except for the chattering and complaining of blue jays, cardinals, and squirrels arguing over territory. Dan looked at her, an unspoken question in his eyes, but she only shook her head, and they moved on. They had gone only a short way when she stopped again, listening. This time when she stopped, the loud snap of a dry branch carried through the trees.

Dan looked in the direction of the sound. "What is it? Another moose?"

"I don't think so. It isn't loud enough or consistent enough to be a moose or bear. Have you heard anything behind us for the last few minutes?"

He shook his head. "No. Did you think you had before that?"

"I'm not sure. It's more of a feeling than anything positive. Never mind, it's probably just my imagination. Let's go."

As they neared the top of the slope, a muffled cry rang out

behind them. The sound of someone falling on the soft forest floor reached them.

They stopped and turned back the way they had come. AJ turned a questioning glance toward Dan. "Animal?" she asked.

"Sounded like a person to me. What'd you think?"

"I don't know, but I've kind of had the feeling we were being followed for a while now."

"Don't suppose there's a chance it could be a search party?"

She shook her head. "No way. They'd be yelling and calling our names every so often. Whoever's back there doesn't want us to know it."

"Get moving." He put her in front of his body and gave her a little push to get her started uphill.

"Stop pushing. It's slick going here."

"If that's who I think it is, we better get to the top of this before he clears the trees, or we'll be in for more than broken bones," he said, dragging her in his wake. "I don't want

to be caught out in the open."

Somberly, AJ nodded and tried to move ahead quicker. When they reached the small peak, they dropped behind a boulder where they could overlook the path below. Within minutes a small figure broke through the brush at the bottom and started to follow their tracks uphill. Sunlight reflected off the metal on the rifle he carried.

Dan groaned and looked around for a sheltered escape route. Finding none, he turned to AJ. "Listen to me and do exactly what I say. I want you to head out over this hill and keep moving south. Without me to slow you down, you should be able to handle the steep slope and make it going straight up. Get over the ridge as quick as you can and head for the river you told me about. I'm going to wait here for him, try and take him out, and then I'll follow you."

Terror at the thought of leaving him, of losing him, gripped her body. Her heart fluttered and a fine sweat popped out on her forehead. AJ opened her mouth to protest.

He cut her off before she could utter a sound. "Aurora, for God's sake, do what I say for a change or neither of us will make it through this. Now get moving." He turned her away and gave her a push in the opposite direction.

Fine. But, if he thinks he can order me around, he's got another think coming. Moving along the ridge line, AJ looked for a vantage point. If Dan thought she was going to leave him to face Stone alone, he had completely misjudged her.

The armed man climbed halfway up the hill, then skirted it to reenter the woods on the far side. AJ could hear him moving through the brush but could no longer see him. Chances were that if she couldn't, neither could Dan. Stone was probably moving around behind him while she sat here doing nothing.

Without a weapon, she was not in a position to help him. Angry at her helplessness, she jumped up and started looking for anything she could use against the man who was stalking them. She found a stout stick and silently moved around Dan, in the opposite direction to the one she thought Stone had taken.

On the far side of the rocks where Dan waited, she sank down on her heels to wait and watch. It seemed like hours, but minutes later, Stone broke out of the brush behind Dan.

"All right. Stand up."

AJ watched in horror as he held the rifle on Dan. Her heart pounded in her ears, and her hands shook as she gripped the stick tighter.

"I said, stand up." He motioned with the rifle. Carefully, Dan rose, turned to face him and raised his hands above his waist.

"Where is she?"

"Look, we didn't mean you any harm. We only used your cabin to get out of the weather. I left some money on the sink for the supplies we used. Why are you doing this?"

Stone waved the rifle at Dan and Dan took a single step back.

"You know who I really am. I know you do. I knew someone would find out sooner or later. You're not the first, you know. Others have come looking for me. I took care of them, too."

"I don't know what you're talking about, Smith."

AJ knew Dan was bluffing, but the man wasn't far enough beyond reason to fall for it.

"You know my name's not Smith. It's Stone, James Stone. Why can't you people just leave me alone? Haven't I been punished enough, living in this God-forsaken wilderness all these years? I've never spent it, you know. Couldn't. People would have known it was stolen."

Curious, Dan asked, "How have you been living if you haven't spent any of the money?"

"Scrimping and doin' without, that's how. I had a small savings I brought with me." He snorted. "The local hicks love to barter, too. I traded elk hides and canned food for other things like flour and coffee." His eyes clouded. "I never touched the money. All this for nothing. I left New York, my fiancé, everything. All for nothing."

"Look, Stone. You could give it back. There's no need to do this. Go back with us and turn yourself in. We'll help you make them see it was all a mistake."

A cackle escaped from the tight lips of the little man. "You're the crazy one. It's worse in prison than up here. No one will ever take me back."

He raised the rifle threateningly. "Now. Where is she?"

Dan shrugged, and Stone motioned with the rifle. "Come on we're going after her."

When the two men turned away from her, AJ jumped up and ran at Stone, the stick raised above her head. Her boots slid on loose shale and snow, drawing the attention of both men as they swung toward her. At the sight of her, Stone raised the rifle and fired. As the gun went off, Dan dove under it and knocked it up and out of Stone's hands, sending the shot harmlessly into the trees. The rifle flew through the air and landed behind a pile of rocks, pillowed in a snowdrift.

Stone turned and jumped on Dan and for a moment AJ froze, watching the scene as though it were a horror movie she couldn't turn away from. Stone had his hands around Dan's throat trying to choke the life from him. Dan's strong hands were on the other man's wrists doing his best to pry him off. The color in Dan's face changed, turning bluish-gray. AJ knew she couldn't wait. Picking up the large piece of wood, she swung it down on top of Stone's head. A cry of pain slipped from his lips as he folded up and fell from Dan's body, rolling over onto his back in the snow.

Dropping to her knees, AJ gently raised Dan's head to her lap brushing his hair back from his forehead as he gasped for breath. "Dan? Dan, are you okay?"

Unable to speak, he simple nodded as he raised a shaky hand to his neck to massage the life back into it. Able to draw enough air through his tight throat to speak, he looked at her, pride and wonder reflected on his face. "Thanks to you I am. Where is he?" he croaked.

"He's still out over there. What are we going to do? Take him back?"

"No. That will slow us down. We'll leave him here and tell the authorities who he is and where we found him. They should be able to back track from where they find us and get to him."

She helped Dan to his feet then bent down to grab the rifle. "This better go with us. Maybe we should search him to be sure this was all he had."

AJ scooped up scattered packs. She hung for a moment in suspended animation. Dan had stopped his search of Stone's pockets and coat. Both gazed into the growing cloud cover. The sound of a plane clearly reached them both. AJ sent him an I-told-you-so look, then an ornery grin. Help would be coming soon. She knew it.

CHAPTER ELEVEN

Dark snow clouds buffeted the small white plane. The flaming bird on the tail looked as though it were flying through a firestorm as the clouds swirled around it then trailed behind like thick smoke. Jorgensen grumbled as the tumbling puffs of gray and black blocked his view of the forest. The heavy moist film was beginning to drop and hang on the statuesque treetops.

 After two days of flying with the rescue effort, he'd begged off on personal business saying it was necessary for him to return to the states. He snickered as he thought of their gullibility. They were all so stupid, it amazed him that any of them stayed in business. After heading south from the airport, he had flown to another Canadian airfield then had doubled back to fly north again on visual flight rules. No one knew where he was.

He headed toward Missisa Lake to check the site of AJ's plane crash. The plane went down. He knew it. He saw it himself. Hadn't he followed them until his devices worked their magic? Everything went according to plan. Before he had flown away, he watched the plane catch fire. It had burned, hadn't it? They must have been caught in it.

He had put the timing devices that had crippled the Beaver on himself. He had long since learned to do dirty jobs himself if he wanted the job done right and for the work to stay confidential. Panic had beads of sweat gathering around the collar of his shirt. He slipped his finger inside it and ran the tip around the circle of fabric. *They couldn't have lived through the crash. Surely not.* If AJ made it back to testify against him, he'd go to prison for sure. With her out of the way, the prosecution's case would fall apart.

When he reached the downed plane he circled, spiraling lower and lower, trying to see through the gathering clouds. When the sky cleared for a moment, he saw it. The red and white plane had not burned. Black streaks reached up its sides like tentacles, but it was intact. The right side of the fuselage was smashed in, but the door on the left side of the plane stood open. *Damn! Did they get out?*

He slammed his fist against the door of the plane. If they'd survived he had to reach them before the others. Had to stop them from making it back. His stomach clutched threatening to make him sick. Taking deep cleansing breaths, he fought to control the feeling of nausea that tried to claim him. His heart pounded wildly as he thought of the consequences of his actions. Money had always been everything to him. To lose it all and have to start over would be devastating. But, it could be worse. The idea of being behind bars terrified him. If AJ continued to pursue his conviction, she was going to uncover enough to have him locked up for a very long time. He couldn't let that happen. There was no doubt—he wouldn't survive in prison.

"We'd better be making a shelter, Dan. This storm looks like it could dump more snow on us, and I, for one, don't care to have my sleeping bag covered with white stuff."

She looked around for a few minutes and found what she sought. A large pine tree with huge arms draping onto the ground from the weight of the snow on its branches. Underneath was a small cave-like space. Setting her pack down she motioned for Dan to do the same.

"Do you think it's a good idea to stop already? What if Stone follows us?"

Her gear landed on the ground. "Surely he won't do that without a weapon or supplies. He'd have to be crazy." She looked at Dan's raised eyebrow. "Okay, point taken, but do you think he's crazy enough to try to take us on when we have the rifle? To risk being caught out here with no food or shelter?"

After a split second, he shook his head. "No, I suppose not. Hopefully he headed home to get what money he could carry and some provisions so he could run."

"Right." Not as convinced as she tried to sound, she propped her pack against the tree.

"You sit down and rest your leg. This won't take long."

"What do you want me to do?"

"I'd rather you take it easy. I want to be at the river tomorrow, and then we'll head east toward Fort Albany. We've still got a ways to go if the searchers don't find us soon."

"Nope. You're tired, too. We'll get this done and both rest. I'll collect fire wood."

When AJ scrounged branches from smaller trees and started piling them around the outside of the shelter on top of the larger branches of the tree she had chosen careful to leave one small hole uncovered.

"Take that last load of wood in, and I'll close us in for now."

Dan ducked through the small opening, dropping his bounty on the small pile he'd already made.

She crawled in through the doorway she'd left in the branches and drew one more bough across the opening to keep out the cold air. Pulling their sleeping bags out of her backpack, AJ spread them out.

"Why don't you lean back against the tree trunk? We can't both move around and work in here. I'm just going to get a fire going."

"Thanks. I'm ready to take you up on that."

She cleared dried pine needles until she could see a bare dirt circle. In the center of it, she carefully stacked dried twigs and bark. Striking a match to the tender, she was satisfied to see the small leap of flames that quickly caught. The needles snapped and crackled, making a lively sound in the stillness of the shelter as rivers of sparks flowed toward the smoke hole in the roof. A small bed of red-hot sticks grew, and she placed larger chunks of wood on the stack until she had a good fire going.

When she looked up, Dan was smiling at her.

"What? What did I do?"

"You're quite a Girl Scout, aren't you?"

Realizing he was teasing her, she shrugged, "I wouldn't knock it. I saved your butt, didn't I? And you'll be plenty glad of this shelter and a warm fire in another few hours. The weather's lookin' pretty wicked out there. We'll have to dig out of here in the morning, but for tonight, we'll be safe and snug."

Dan laughed and reached out to grab her and pull her toward him before she could dodge. She fell back across his legs, grabbing his shoulders to steady herself as she landed.

"Saved my butt, huh?" He looked at her laughing face. "Well, maybe you did," he whispered. His warm ungloved hand slipped to the side of her face in a soft caress. "How do you think I can repay that?"

The familiar scent of wintergreen enveloped her as the thought of tasting it on his tongue stole her breath away. His gaze locked with hers, making it impossible to look away. When he released her eyes, her wandering gaze dropped to his lips. A smile tweaked at the corners of his mouth before it disappeared and a thoughtful look replaced it.

When she could draw air again, it froze in her lungs. Her heart stopped, ceasing to beat for what felt like several seconds. His lips were a dangerous sight, so she slowly raised her eyes to his, looking for answers to unasked questions. Unable to withstand the power of his look, she watched his eyes as she surrendered her lips to his. The sparkle of laughter they shared moments before was replaced by something deeper, something lasting.

Their lips joined, and her heart started beating again, this time pounding down the home stretch like a runaway racehorse. Dan drew his good leg up under her to support her upper body and to hold her closer. Her head dropped back against his upper arm as his teeth nipped at her throat, exploring the taste and feel of her. Bringing her head back up, she nuzzled against his throat, feeling his pulse throbbing against her lips. She took a deep breath and tried futilely for a moment of sanity.

AJ pulled air into her lungs and caught the male scent of his body. It seemed to meld perfectly with that of the outdoors, of pine and snow and moss.

"Dan..."

"If you want me to stop, Aurora, say it now. Otherwise I'm going to love you. I said you couldn't run forever, but I won't do anything you don't want me to. Aurora? Tell me what you want me to do."

When her gaze met his, she knew she had to take things as they came. AJ lifted her hands to sink them in the waves that drifted around his face. A moment's fear slipped through her. *Could she love him and then watch him go back to Chicago?* Love him. That was what she wanted to do. The rest would come in time if it was meant. Firmly, at last sure of what she needed, she pulled his face back down to hers. A breath away from him she stopped, her lips separated from his by only a whisper.

"Love me, Dan. Completely and without promises we might not be able to keep."

Their mouths came together, searching, desperate and hungry. The frustration of several days of pent-up emotions brought an urgency to them. As Dan drew her closer to his side, the kiss deepened and became demanding. He started to unzip her jacket. With her lips locked to his, AJ's hands pushed impatiently at the fabric of his flannel shirt, pulling the western snaps apart to slip her hands inside against his bare flesh. His groan was swallowed by her as he slipped her jacket from her shoulders, breaking the contact with her lips only long enough to lay the coat behind them. Leaning against it, he kissed her eyes, trailing his lips from the closed long-lashed lids over her cheeks as his nimble fingers unfastened the buttons of her shirt.

When his fingers were finally able to reach inside her blouse and found the lace garment beneath, he pulled his lips away from hers. This woman he loved was a collage of contrasts, wool and lace, leather boots and silken beauty. He wrapped his fingers in the dainty material hidden beneath the woolen shirt.

His hands slipped the fabric away to tease her breast. Her breath caught in her throat as little purring sounds escaped, driving Dan closer to the edge. Pushing her shirt aside, he slowly unfastened the ties that held her camisole closed. One by one, they slipped free of their bows. She held her breath as the last one fell open at her waist. Dan drew the narrow strap down as he kissed her bare shoulder, then moved lower to kiss the soft swell of her breast.

Dan slipped the material away from first one side then the other to gaze at her body. His hands slipped to the side of her rib cage below her breasts, holding her, caressing her. He looked down on her body unashamed as she blushed softly. "You're beautiful, Aurora," he whispered. "So beautiful. I could never have enough of you."

He buried his face between her breasts, taking in the soft curves of them and the scent of her skin.

She gripped the wavy mass of his hair holding his face against her pounding heart. Firelight bounced off the red and gold highlights in the dim light of the shelter.

Impatient to feel his skin against her, she fumbled with the tails of his shirt until she could pull it from the waistband of his pants. Her lips found his again as she ran her hand over

the rippling muscles of his chest. Dragging her mouth from his, AJ lowered her lips to travel across his chest then over his nipples as he had her own. When she closed her lips over him, nipping playfully at the light brown tip, a gasp exploded from his lips. He pulled her back up to capture her lips again. When she reached for his mouth, the tips of her breasts brushed against the hair on his chest sending shivers of delight through her body.

Male strength radiated between his thighs as he laid her back on their sleeping bags. She watched, her gaze locked on his heated one as he lowered his head to her breast and circled one peak with his lips, gently tugging its already erect shape. Deep in the pit of her stomach, her muscles twisted and turned, longing for a release of the tension rapidly growing within her.

When Dan lowered his hand to the top of her jeans to release the snap that kept him form reaching her most intimate parts, AJ slipped beyond reason. As eager as he to lie skin to skin, flesh to flesh, she opened the closure to his slacks and helped him from his clothes just as he helped her. Dan gathered her to his breast as he ran his hands up and down her bare back.

As she lay at his side his hands caressed her in a way she'd allowed no one else. His warm palm slipped up and down her thigh, teasing and driving her closer to the edge. The nerve endings in her body vibrated at the touch of his hands moments before they came together as one, oblivious to the wind and blowing snow surrounding their hide-away.

CHAPTER TWELVE

The silence in the cabin of the Queen Air seemed as thick as London fog. The sun sank in the western sky, obliterated by a screen of growing storm clouds. A dark blanket resembling the puffy squares of a down comforter and laden with snow settled across the sky.

Roy gazed uselessly into the dense clouds, praying for a break in the shroud below, praying for a glimpse of anything that would lead them to AJ and Dan. He watched Marjorie sit, her hands wound together in her lap, her spine stiff, staring helplessly toward the earth beneath them. As the tallest tree was engulfed in the sinking weight of the heavy clouds, a tear slipped silently from her eye and slid unchecked down her cheek. The somber mood in the plane seemed to reflect the approaching storm front as Roy turned his attention back to the barely visible ground.

"Ben." Roy drew the pilot's attention, his voice flat. "Let's go back. We'll have to re-fly this strip when the weather lifts."

With a deep sigh, Ben clamped his jaw shut, nodded his agreement, and turned the plane south. A short time later, the Queen Air circled the airfield and came in for a soft touchdown

just as large scattered snowflakes materialized and began striking
the windshield. By the time the plane reached the end of the
runway, the flakes poured from the sky, covering the plane and
the blacktop in a fresh coating of white powder.

A slim man in a dark trench coat stood in the open doorway
of the hangar. A snap-brim hat was pulled over his eyes. Roy
watched the man flick a still burning cigarette into the new snow
creating a red arc against the darkening sky. He looked like a
private eye from the '40s. Roy halfway expected to recognize
Bogie's features when the man turned toward them. The man
was a stranger to him, yet it was obvious he was waiting for their
plane. Roy sent a puzzled look at Geoffrey Satterfield.

"Friend of yours?"

"Not exactly. Name's Schmidt," Geoffrey said. "He's the
private investigator I use from time to time."

Roy chuckled as he watched the PI. "What'd he do, train by
watching the *Maltese_Falcon*?"

"No," Satterfield snapped. "And, he's very good at what he does.
He's done several odd jobs for me. I had him checking out your
suspicions of Jorgensen." He glanced at Marjorie, then leaned close
to Roy. "He's checked on Marjorie over the last twenty years."

"You had your ex-wife followed?" Roy exclaimed.

"Quiet, damn it. I just had him make sure she was all right."

Roy watched the expression on the other man's face, watched
his glances at the woman he claimed to not care about. "Seems
strange to go to so much bother for an ex-wife?"

"She's the mother of my son," Geoffrey said. "Was I supposed
to leave her twisting in the wind?"

"No, but some would have."

Geoffrey straightened up with a harrumph. Roy smiled. *The
old boy isn't as tough as he wants us to think.*

"You go on in where it's warm." Geoffrey told the group.
"I'll find out what he knows and be right there."

They all muttered agreements and gladly slipped into the heat of the airfield office. It took only a few minutes, then Geoffrey joined them inside cutting straight to the information he had just received.

"Schmidt had a little trouble tracking Jorgensen's personal moves because he's using the company plane, but he found proof he flew up here the day AJ and Dan started out. And even though he begged off from the search and rescue operation to head south, he is still here and landing at an airfield twenty miles from here."

"Just what I thought," Roy said. "I bet he sabotaged the plane, and now he's afraid we'll find it or else that they survived to talk about it."

"Just what the hell is going on, Roy? Why would a stranger want to murder my son?"

"Unfortunately, he took a ride with the wrong pilot. He doesn't even care about Dan. He's after AJ."

"What could he have done that's bad enough to compound it with murder?" Marjorie asked.

"He defrauded a lot of people in our town. Caused many of 'em to go bankrupt and lose their homes. We would have if it hadn't been for AJ wising up to him and going after a prosecution case. He's got to keep her from getting back to finalize everything and testify against him."

Roy sat and thought for a minute as he unconsciously rocked back and forth in his chair. If Jorgensen caused the plane crash, were they still alive? Why would he be up here if he didn't suspect they had made it out of the crash and could pin it on him? When he spoke again there was more hope in his voice than had been there for days. It was tainted by the sound of fear, but it was there.

"My guess is, we follow him tomorrow morning, and he'll lead us right to them. If not to them, to the wreck and that will give us a heading to try and track them. Can Schmidt work for you tomorrow?"

"With the retainer I give him, he can work for me anytime. What's the plan?"

"Let's have Schmidt near the private airfield with a radio. When Jorgensen takes off he can let us know and give us a heading. We'll take off from here and come in behind Jorgensen

and follow him north. I want to let the police know what's going on and see if they'll send someone with us tomorrow."

Inside the pine tree hut, AJ and Dan lay wrapped in each other's arms, the sleeping bag pulled over their bare bodies. A small fire in the center of the evergreen cave gave them all the warmth they needed to add to their body heat.

AJ reached up and curled her fingers in his hair twisting a strand around her fingertip. She had never known anyone raised in wealth or in a large city. Curious, she wanted to know more about Dan's background and his family life, but she wasn't sure he wanted to talk about either. She bit the inside of her lip, then took a chance that he wouldn't withdraw from her after what they had shared earlier.

"Dan?"

"Hmm?"

"We talked about my mother. Why don't you ever talk about yours?"

He shifted a lazy smile toward her and scooted her around so he could see her face. "No reason. It just hadn't really come up. Her name's Marjorie, and she's beautiful. Almost as beautiful as you," he added. "I'll take you to meet her when we get out of this."

AJ noted that his eyes looked warm and loving, pride clear in his expression when he spoke of his mother.

"My folks divorced when I was twelve. I stayed with my dad."

Pain shafted into her, twisting her stomach into knots. A boy without his mother through the teen years? How awful was that? At least she'd had her mother until she was an adult.

Dan continued but not before a flash of pain flickered across his features temporarily replacing the look of pride and love.

"When I turned eighteen, Mom felt it was time to approach me to talk about what had happened."

"She stayed away all that time with no contact at all?" AJ failed to keep the incredulous tone from her voice, and thought she could easily understand the pain she had seen on Dan's face.

"Yeah. But we got together later and got things all straightened out. We see each other every month or so." He shook his head, the hair falling across his forehead like a boy's. "Dad doesn't know." Slipping his arm closer around AJ, he drew her against his body as one hand caressed her thigh. She grabbed his hand to stop its roving.

"Why on earth doesn't he know about it? What could it hurt?"

Dan shrugged against her. "He has a real hard time admitting it was his fault their marriage hit the skids. He was infatuated with a secretary more than twenty years ago and had a short affair with her. Mom found out and walked out on him. Dad seemed to think she should have forgiven him, and it was her fault they split."

AJ looked at him with disbelief. "You're kidding me, right?"

"No, but he's since figured out that's not the way it works. Dad was bitter for a long time, though. Sometimes I'm not sure he's over it yet."

"How so?"

"Instead of a real marriage, he married the company. It's all he has besides me, and he used me as an excuse to keep away from her."

"You can't live his life for him. He made choices, and not very good ones. If you want to go back, that's fine. But you have to make choices just as he did."

"I'm beginning to see that. He wrapped himself in the company because he really couldn't forgive himself, plus he had too much pride to go to her and admit he was wrong and that he still loved her."

AJ thought of her father. Of the love he still carried for her mother that was as strong as the day she'd died.

"Does he still?"

Dan pulled her close as she spoke, bending his head to brush his lips across her forehead before nuzzling her hair against his face. His day-old beard caught at the soft strands before they drifted away to be caught in his fingers.

"Still what?"

AJ pushed away from him. "Love her. Does he still love her after all this time?"

Dan looked down into her eyes. She knew her eyes were filled with sentimental tears. It was her curse. He chuckled before he drew her close again. "I don't know, Aurora, but if I know you like I think I do, we're going to find out. We'll just have to find a way to bring them together. Right now we have more pressing things to worry about."

With his finger under her chin, he raised her face to his. His breath whispered over her lips a heartbeat before the moist warmth of his brushed across her mouth. His teeth nipped at her lower lip before he drew the fullness of it into his mouth. A groan of pure rapture slipped from her. AJ wondered if she could die from an overdose of ecstasy.

Dragging his lips from hers, Dan slipped lower, his tongue stroking her body. His kisses roamed to the peaks of her tingling breasts then slipped lower still. The clasping of her fingers in his hair encouraged him to go on with his explorations. She hoped he would introduce her to all of the varied delights she had not yet experienced. As his hands slipped around her body to draw them together again, AJ surrendered to the sensual pleasure of his touch.

***

Cursing the rapidly falling snow, Jorgensen had at first refused to give up. Finally, accepting the futility of searching in the growing blizzard, he headed south toward his friend's landing field at Dog Lake.

The windshield wipers swished from side to side removing the mounting snow as quickly as it gathered. Suddenly, he sat up leaning closer to the glass. He wiped the condensation from the inside where the defroster was having trouble keeping up with the moisture in the cockpit. Peering out over the nose of the plane, he hoped he was right. Mixed in with the storm clouds was a tiny column of smoke off to his west. Diving closer he buzzed the treetops barely clearing the white tops with the belly of his plane.

"Yes!" Elated, he circled twice more to be sure. The smoke seemed to be coming from under a pile of snow or from the center of a tree. He couldn't tell which in the growing clouds and swirling snow. Surely, nobody else was crazy enough to be camped out here in this storm. It had to be them.

Leveling the plane out, he took down his exact location and headed due south to the Fort Albany River to scout a landing site before heading on to Dog Lake. He'd have to borrow an amphibious plane. And a gun. When this storm lifted he vowed, he'd be back and AJ MacKenzie would be out of his hair for good.

AJ lay back against their bedrolls, laughing at Dan. He was rolling around on his blanket trying to pull on his pants. All he succeeded in doing was twisting up in the bedding, becoming hopelessly tangled.

"Darn it, AJ, don't just lay there. We have to get outside so they can see us."

"I'm telling you, it won't do any good. By the time you get out there, the plane will be gone. Even if it isn't, whoever is in it won't see you through this storm. If they see anything at all it will be the smoke from the fire, and they'll be back as soon as the storm breaks to check it out."

Dan stopped struggling as he listened to her arguments and lay barefoot and bare chested with his pants on but not fastened. The sleeping bag wrapped around his calves capturing him. He fought the fabric. "Blast it all to hell!"

A smile crept across her face causing her lips to tremble as she pulled back the cover, shamelessly revealing what she had to offer him in addition to her heart.

"Are you that anxious to get rescued, Dan?"

He looked across at her body, gleaming in the soft firelight. She saw the muscles across his chest tighten and vibrate as he sucked in his breath. A smile tugged at the corners of his mouth as he let his gaze travel the length of her from her ebony hair to her toes and back again. He gave an exaggerated sigh.

"Well..."

"Think about it, Dan." Her voice was sultry and heavy with longing. "Are you really eager to go home? Our vacation would be over." She tried to keep her tone light, but she felt like unseen hands wrapped around her lungs and twisted the air from them like so much water from a wet towel. Did she want this vacation to end? Could she bear to lose him to his business?

She could see he was already responding to her invitation.

"I guess not. Tomorrow or the next day, maybe next week would be soon enough." Kicking his legs free, he slipped out of his pants. He scooted over to draw her back into the circle of his arms. "Maybe never would be okay, too. You're the survivalist. How long could you keep us alive up here on moss soup and love?" His mouth covered hers before she could answer.

The fire between them burst into spontaneous flame, and they became lost in each other again.

***

Roy's gaze slid around the airfield café where he and the others sat at a Formica topped table. Pictures of World War I and II planes graced the dingy pink walls, some hanging drunkenly on nails. Empty white stoneware, chipped and stained from thousands of meals and coffee thick enough to cut with a knife, sat on the table.

His unfinished the coffee had grown cold and bitter as they enthusiastically made plans for the next day. The information from Schmidt gave them all reason to renew their hope. They didn't think Jorgensen would be in Canada if he knew AJ and Dan were already dead. At least now, they had a good idea of why the plane went down, if not how. Roy knew that if anyone could put the plane down safely in the wild, it was AJ.

Geoffrey reached out and snagged the check before the others could protest. Everyone moved away from the table as he took care of the bill.

Roy watched with amusement as Marjorie's gaze locked like a homing device onto Satterfield's long lean body. She was obviously enjoying the view as he took determined strides across the cafe. When she looked back toward Roy, her cheeks were flushed a delightful shade of rose. He doubted it was from the cheap wine they'd had with dinner.

"How about a nightcap, Roy?" Geoffrey asked when he rejoined them. "You're all welcome to join us back at the hotel," he said, his look taking in the entire group.

Roy looked at him for a moment before he answered. Marjorie was standing close, very close to Geoffrey's side. Although they weren't touching, they seemed bound together just the same. The longer the two were together, the more tangible the tension between them became. They had been sending sparks off each other all day. Roy wasn't sure whether the pressure would erupt in hostility or seduction. Either way, he didn't care to be a witness to it.

"I can't speak for the others, but I'm bushed." A quick survey showed nodding heads all around. "Thanks anyway, Geoffrey. I think we'll turn in and see you in the morning.

We're all set on what's going down?" At Geoffrey's nod, he continued. "Good. Thanks for dinner. We'll see you tomorrow. Good night, Marjorie." Roy nodded to her then spun around with practiced ease and rolled away from the couple.

Marjorie and Geoffrey stepped into their suite. He helped her slide out of her coat and hung it in the foyer closet before moving to the fireplace in the living room. He lit the small fire he'd laid before they left that morning. Moving to a built-in stereo, he played with the stations until he found the haunting and melodious sounds of James Galway's flute.

He straightened from the cabinet and faced her. "Sherry?" he asked quietly.

She simply inclined her head, stood and gathered warmth from the fire, her hands rubbing up and down her arms. Geoffrey handed her a tiny flute filled with amber liquid, and moved to sit on the love seat in front of the hearth. Marjorie moved past him and sat in an armchair at one end of it.

"Afraid of me, Marjorie? I won't bite, you know."

"I know exactly what you're capable of, in case you've forgotten." She smiled gently and settled deeper in the overstuffed chair.

She slipped off her boots and curled her legs up into the chair beside her, tucking her feet beneath her body. The unconscious move brought a warm smile to Geoffrey's mouth. He remembered the gesture from many evenings spent sitting and reading or listening to classical music. Marjorie had rarely sat with her feet on the floor and her shoes on. She had always been barefoot and always sat cross-legged or with her feet hidden beneath her.

"Why do you do that?"

"What?" Puzzled she stopped her glass a breath away from her lips, then continued to sip sherry as he pointed to her feet.

"That. You've always insisted on sitting on your feet."

She shifted self-consciously and shrugged. "I just do. It's a bad habit."

"There's nothing wrong with it. I just wondered why you do it."

She gave a disgusted sigh. "My feet are ugly, okay? I was always trying to hide them from the other girls when I was a child, and I got in the habit of sitting like this because I found it comfortable."

Geoffrey surveyed the still beautiful hair, body and hands of his ex-wife. Thought of her determination to come and search for her son. *What the hell did I lose by letting her go?*

"There is nothing about you that is ugly, Marjorie." Geoffrey didn't move from the love seat, but he caressed her just the same. His eyes, his voice. He touched her without getting close. He let his gaze travel from her shining hair to her bare tucked-up feet stroking her body along the way.

"You are the most beautiful woman I have ever had the pleasure to look at, among the other things I have had the profound pleasure to do to you."

A sincere smile lifted the corners of his mouth and brought a small dimple to his left cheek.

Marjorie sucked in her breath and Geoffrey's hopes soared at her reaction.

She sipped from her glass, and her hand shook sending some of her drink over the crystal edge and into her lap. She set the glass down, being careful not to spill more, and gracefully rose to her feet as she brushed off the front of her slacks. When Geoffrey started to rise and come to her, she held out her hand gesturing for him to stay in his seat. She backed away from him, shaking her head.

His voice stopped her retreat. "It's obvious we still feel something very special for each other. Give me another chance— give us another chance." He coaxed.

"Don't ask that of me, Geoffrey. This is too much, too soon. We have a physical attraction to each other that's as strong today as it was twenty years ago. But, nothing has

changed. We're still divorced."

"Maybe you should have stayed away then."

"You know I couldn't do that. Let's make a pact. We find our son first. Then, if you want to see me, I would be glad to go out with you, and we'll see how things go."

At that Geoffrey was on his feet. "Go out? On a date? We're not a couple of high school kids."

"That may be, but we've changed, Geoffrey, both of us. I'll not jump back into bed with you because you have the power to abolish my sense of what's right and wrong with one of your smiles."

His voice was soft and deep. "We loved each other once, may still. We had a child together. What could be wrong about our being together again?"

"It isn't only that we're no longer married. I can be as progressive as the next woman. We need to get to know each other again first. To be sure it's right." Her voice grew quiet as

her eyes lowered, slipping away from his piercing look. "I have to be sure I can trust you. I won't share you with another woman anymore now than I was willing to before."

A brief flicker of pain and guilt raced across his face before he hid it. For the first time he truly felt regret at what he had done to her. What he had made her feel all those long years ago.

"I'm sorry for what I did to us then, but we're still attracted to each other, Marjorie. I know you can feel it just as much as I do."

He advanced toward her, but she continued to back away and ducked behind the sofa to put a barrier between them.

"Do you want to win me back or are you looking for a quick fix for the guilt you feel over our marriage?"

His jaw tightened, a tiny muscle at the base twitching.

"I thought so. You aren't sure are you? First we find Dan, then we'll sort this out if you still want to. Good night, Geoffrey." Her head held high, shoulders straight, she spun on her bare heel and crossed the thick carpet to her room. Marjorie closed the door behind her with a firm snap.

Geoffrey tossed back the remains of his drink, trying desperately to quench the fire that was burning deep within his body. She had always had the power to turn him into a quivering schoolboy lost in lust. *Damn it, is it lust or do I still love her?* Was love still possible after all these years? After what he'd done to her?

If she could stay in control, then he could, too. She wasn't going to have him crawling and begging for mercy. At least not any time soon.

His gut instincts told him his boy was alive. They'd find him sooner or later. He smiled as he thought out a plan. First they had to find Dan, then he would mount a campaign to find out the depth of his feelings for Marjorie and hers for him. When he slipped into his own room, he was aroused and tied in knots by the desire he felt for his ex-wife. Sleep would be slow in coming this night.

CHAPTER THIRTEEN

AJ shivered in the pre-dawn air. She lay against Dan so the bare curve of her back fit perfectly against the front of his body. Their breath came in visible little bursts of steam.

She ran the tips of her fingers up and down the muscled arm thrown across her body, his hand resting gently on the firm swell of one breast. The mat of hair on his chest, and the shorter prickly hair scattered over his thighs, excited the nerve endings of her sensitive skin where their bodies met. During the night, they had made love several times. He had been at once gentle yet demanding; fulfilled yet insatiable. She had been as ravenous as he. Even after a night filled with intermittent passion, the closeness of his body tightened the muscles of her own. Anticipation of another intimate coupling kicked her pulse into high gear.

The pine boughs sagging under the weight of snow insulated their shelter. In spite of that, the close contact and heat radiating between their bodies failed to keep the early morning air from infiltrating and chilling their cozy hideaway. Dan's steady rhythmic breathing fluttered across her neck lifting the hair at the base of her head as it sent shivers up her spine. Sliding out from under his hand, she propped up on her elbow to reach out and stir the embers of the fire.

Dan moaned and shifted on the blanket as he tried to pull her back. She felt him shudder and assumed a rush of freezing air hit his chest where she had been shielding it with her body.

"Just a second, Dan. I have to stoke this fire up a bit."

AJ chuckled as he groaned and tried again to pull her back as she slapped his hands away. At last successful in rekindling the almost dead fire, she tucked her body against the welcoming curve of his and pulled the cover back over them. They seemed made to fit together like this, she thought. It seemed so natural, so right. "It is," her heart whispered. Now she wasn't so reluctant to listen to her little voice. The voice of her heart.

Flames rose up, lapping at the dry wood and sending a tiny column of sparks floating into the air like bubbles reaching for the surface of a glass of champagne. Still half asleep, Dan reached over her and gently fondled her breast. The smoothness of his hands reminded her he was a city man, the vice-president of a major corporation no less. Yet his body was as tightly toned as a track star. Whether in a boardroom or on a handball court, she was sure he would exude power and control. The image was exciting, but could she spend her life in Chicago? AJ sighed softly as she reminded herself that he hadn't asked her to, so that wasn't an issue.

She shook her head. It was hopeless anyway. She'd never leave her father. Without her, Sky Dancer Aeronautics was dead. She couldn't kill something her father cared so much about.

The beating of Dan's heart against her back brought her thoughts back to the moment, to the feel of his body against hers. Tiny electric charges snapped in the air each time they touched.

Was it the heat from the fire that turned her blood to liquid fire and sent it coursing through her veins? Or was it the delight his touch shot straight to the core of her soul? When his fingers teased first one already tense peak and then the other, she snuggled back to get closer to his body. His arousal rested against her slim hip. A smile curved the corners of her lips. She loved the power she held over his body. The power that could bring such an immediate and complete response. His heart throbbed against her back where they lay pressed together.

Dan slipped an arm under her to draw her into the circle of his arms trying to meld their bodies as one. He crossed his arms in front of her body as he bent his head to nibble on the sensitive cord of muscle that ran from her shoulder to the base of her throat. His lips trailed up to nip gently on the lobe of her ear where he pulled her hair aside. Wave after wave of expectation rolled through her, growing like a tsunami that hits shore after an ocean bottom eruption.

Her breath came in sharp gasps as Dan once again lifted her breast in his large palm and slipped his other hand down over the creamy skin of her stomach. Her muscles tightened as she sucked in her breath, drawing her buttocks back against his flat abdomen when she did. She shivered as she pressed back against him while he explored her throat and the underside of her jaw when she tried to face him. When she slipped her hand down the length of his thigh to the back of his knee, she felt him quiver against her hips as he drew his leg up and over hers to trap her.

"Dan," she whispered. Turning in his arms she came to him eager for his touch, greedy for love. There was no hesitation, no thought of what might be right or wrong, no thought of the next hour or day or year. She acknowledged her love for him and drew him into herself ready to accept whatever he could find in his heart to give her.

A short time later, they lay content in each other's arms. Both were covered with a fine sheen of perspiration. The musty odor of lovemaking mixed with the scents of pine and wood smoke. AJ looked at him, a wicked smile tweaking her lips.

"All you want me for is a sex slave, Mr. Satterfield." She tucked her tongue into her cheek. "Sky Dancer Aeronautics doesn't provide that particular service."

His smile faded and a contemplative expression replaced it. He gently cupped her cheek in his palm. "I won't say I don't enjoy your body. You're beautiful and giving, but there is so much more, AJ."

Her smile faded and a lump grew in her throat.

"Imagine all we could do together, trips up here and other places around the world. Think of the fun we could have. Of the love we could share." He gazed directly into her eyes. "What do you say, AJ?"

This is getting too heavy too fast. AJ fought to lighten the mood again. It would do no good to know he loved her. It would only make it harder to let him go.

"I'll melt some snow on the fire if you want to wash up. It's kind of tricky with only one small pan of hot water, but it can be done. I could help you and you could help me." Assuming he would be willing, she turned and threw aside the cover to reach for a cup. As she stooped down to reach outside and scoop up some of the fresh snow, he gave her rump a playful slap.

She gasped and swung around, sailing a fistful of snow, hitting him in the face and filling his mouth with the freezing crystals as he laughed at her. "What's so funny?"

"I had no idea when I hired you to 'fly me' that you were such a temptress and just what kind of flying you could do."

AJ tossed her long hair over her bare back. "You haven't seen anything yet." She hesitated, tipping her head to one side as her expression became serious.

"Do you mind, Dan?" she asked, her voice still husky from lovemaking.

"Mind what, AJ?" Dan had a silly grin on his face as he looked at her with one brow raised. Obviously they weren't on the same plane.

"A strong-willed woman who attacks your body, routinely," she said dodging the real issue.

"Aurora, nothing you do is routine. Besides, do I look like I mind?" He grinned at her.

Ducking back from the doorway, she pretended to assess his features a frown of concentration on her face. She set the cup beside the fire so the snow would melt and tipped her head to the side, her long hair falling within his reach.

"You look like the most contented man I ever saw."

Something flashed in his eyes sending a flicker of fear shafting through her heart, her breathing brought to a standstill as her throat constricted.

He reached out and curled his fist into her hair dragging her down on the bedroll with him. She stopped so that his face stayed a sigh away from her lips. "You'd better never see another man as contented as I am right now." He smiled as he said it making it not sound like an order but more like a request. He drew her into a soul-stealing kiss. The kiss devoured her mouth bringing them closer than even their lovemaking had done. She responded without hesitation gladly surrendering herself to his caresses. The pressure of his mouth began to change, to seduce. She could no longer breath when at last he freed her so she could sit back on her heels.

She looked at his firm chest, the tight muscles covered with fine hair. Beneath the skin on his throat, she could see his pulse throbbing with promise. Her gaze roamed slowly, appreciatively down his body. Below the blanket that covered his nakedness, she could see signs of his arousal. The thought of what he had done to her body and what he could do again brought heat to her cheeks and a flutter of expectation to her stomach.

With trembling hands, she reached across her pack and pulled a small bandanna from her jeans' pocket. Slowly waving it in front of him, she cocked one eyebrow. "Ready to wash up?"

He laughed, then caught her and dragged her down beside him. As she landed, butt first on the hard ground, she let out a startled yelp. "You first," he said, dragging the cloth from her fingers. "Allow me." As he dipped it into the warmed water, she didn't argue.

Washed up and dressed, Dan stepped out of the shelter for a minute while AJ threw together a quick breakfast. Twenty feet from their hut lay a bundle of cloth mostly covered by drifting snow. Curious, he moved cautiously toward the pile.

"Jeez..." Dan stooped beside the still form wrapped in a frozen jacket. Snow and ice crusted the shaggy eyebrows and stubby whiskers. The skin was blue and lifeless, but Dan recognized the face anyway. Stone lay against the tree trunk appearing to sleep. A quick check of his pulse confirmed for Dan that this wasn't the case. The left hand of the corpse was wrapped around a leather-sheathed knife. The other hand clutched the lapels of his coat at his throat as though trying to hoard the warmth of his body. It hadn't worked.

"Greed, nothing but pure greed." Disgust with the waste of the man's life brought him to his feet. Had he killed others to protect the fortune he was terrified to spend? Were the bodies in the mine shaft that nearly claimed AJ's life?

How absurd life could be. It was finished now. Stone had spent his life seeking something illusive and relative, wealth. He had defined it by the amount of money he had. And he had lost it all. Dan used different criteria. A good woman was one of those, and he didn't intend to let her slip through his fingers. Like his father had let his mother get away.

Not wanting AJ to see the body, Dan gripped the shoulders of Stone's jacket and scooted him back into the brush. There weren't enough rocks to cover the body, and they had no shovel. A burial would have to wait for the police.

He waited until they had finished breakfast before telling AJ of his grisly discovery. When they were ready to head out he spoke up. "AJ?"

Puzzled by his protective tone, she turned an inquiring gaze on him. "What? Aren't you ready to go?"

"Yeah. I don't know how to say this except straight out. Stone caught up with us last night."

Fear flashed across her face before it was controlled. "Is he still out there?"

"He is, but he won't be bothering us or anyone else again. He's dead."

"Dead! But how? I didn't hear anything last night."

"Looks to me like he fell in some water. His clothes were frozen solid. Instead of turning back, he came after us. He had a knife hidden on him somewhere, because it's still gripped in his hand."

"I thought he'd gone back," she said with a sigh. "What a stupid waste."

"It seems pretty barbaric to leave him lying there, but I don't think we should take time to bury him."

"You're right. We should get out of here while we can. It'd take hours to break through the snow and dirt without a shovel. We'll send the police back after we get out."

Dan thought about what might be left of Stone if a bear or mountain lion got to him before that. With a shudder, he shook the image away. "I don't like it, but it's more important for us to get out of here alive than to worry about a dead man."

Picking up their gear, they headed out hoping to reach the river later in the morning. The clouds cleared away and the warming temperatures melted the snow where the sun struck the ground between the trees. They had been walking a couple of hours when they came to a large creek.

They scouted the area along the rushing water. It looked like foaming root beer where it cavorted around huge boulders and bubbled into lather. The rocks were too far apart to serve as steppingstones. Caught between the shores against a huge chunk of granite was a solid looking log.

"Here, Dan. This looks pretty secure. Let's walk across on it. Let me get over, then you follow."

"Right."

Approaching the fallen tree, she sank knee deep in a grass-covered hole. As she lost her balance, Dan grabbed her elbow and stopped her fall. When he pulled her up and out of the small cavity, she cursed the unexpected opening.

"Whoa! Steady there. You okay?"

"Yeah, just wasn't paying enough attention."

"What is that, a gopher hole or something?"

"It's a beaver entrance. Look down there where the water's backing up."

Dan followed her gaze and quickly recognized the beaver dam and hut. "I've seen lots of these on hunting trips, but never paid too much attention. Do they go into it from here?"

"Here and lots of other places. I'm sure there'll be lots more of these holes so watch your step. We don't need you twisting your knee again."

"I'm not the one who almost fell flat on my face." He gave her a smug grin as she frowned at him and turned toward the log.

Their makeshift bridge lay in a shadowed area. A layer of snow and heavy frost from the night before turned the twelve inch round surface as slippery as new soles on a freshly waxed floor. Balanced precariously, AJ inched across placing one foot gingerly in front of the other. The log rested a few feet above the creek. The distance over was relatively short, and she was able to keep her balance to reach the other side of the stream without being dunked.

"Be careful. The frost hasn't melted yet. If you fall, don't fight it or you might really mangle your knee. Keep your eyes up and just ease across."

Dan gave her a crooked little grin. "I have crossed creeks before." His confidence was justified and moments later he jumped off the end of the log and stood beside her.

She gave him a cocky little bow. "Point taken, Mr. Satterfield." AJ grinned and set off across the deep grass growing at the water's edge.

"It's beautiful here isn't it? It always smells so fresh around these streams. The grass is covered with frost and heavy dew. The scent mixes with pine and autumn leaves. I wouldn't ever want to be very far from it," she added quietly.

Dan laughed at her enthusiasm. "I suspect you're the kind that loves to smell a freshly squashed skunk or a feedlot. I can hear you now 'Fresh country air, isn't it great'." He imitated her sucking in a huge breath of outdoor air. When he got his belly full, it stuck out over his belt. Without warning AJ reached over and punched him, deflating his stomach like a burst balloon.

"Make fun of me, will you." She laughed and gave him a jab in the ribs with her elbow just for good measure. He held up his hands in surrender. "Just kidding, AJ. I agree with you. The scent of the forest is better than any scent you can buy in a bottle, that's for sure." When she shot him a disbelieving gaze, he continued. "Honestly, it's better than any of the flowery junk some women like to wear."

"Right. Watch out for this hole," she called out over her shoulder when she saw another beaver opening hidden under the thick weeds. As she spoke, she sidestepped it to avoid falling. Her foot sank through the dense damp vegetation beside the hollow. Before she reached solid ground, the sound of screeching metal shrieked through the forest. She screamed out in agony as steel jaws clamped shut on her ankle making her stumble.

Dan hurried to her side as she threw her gear down and dropped to the ground, grabbing at the trap that held her foot. Her face was linen white, and she bit down on her lip. She kept still as Dan attempted to free her.

"Hang on, honey. I'll get this off. Just sit tight and let me pry it open." He pushed down on the mechanism with the butt of Stone's rifle. Nothing happened. The rusted metal refused to budge. Each time he tried again, AJ's face changed shades from gray to green and back again. He had to repeat the effort several times before the frozen trap gave way, and the jaws pulled back from the chewed leather of her hiking boot.

As her leg came free, AJ gasped in pain and fell away from the trap. Her hands shook as she clasped her injured ankle.

"Just what we need. How are we going to walk out now?" A stream of highly creative words followed her question.

Dan let her rant as he eased her back and stretched her leg out in front of her. "First things first. Let's see how bad it is, then we'll figure out what to do."

He unlaced her boot and spread the sides of it as far open as possible. "Hang on. This is going to burn like hell."

Dan pulled her foot free. AJ cried out and shuddered. She sat up but taking her shoulders in his hands, Dan forced her down onto her pack. Sweat gathered on her body.

Dan pulled her sock aside. Jagged teeth marks marred her flesh. Fabric clung to the gaping wounds. Fury flooded into him, clouding his capacity to reason. How could someone use a trap like this? How could they walk away and leave it like a ticking time bomb waiting for the first innocent person or animal that gets too close?

Barely able to suppress his rage, he checked her ankle for breaks. He found an uneven piece of bone under her skin. Glancing at her face, he saw sweat beaded above her lips, lips turned white from being pressed together in pain. He carefully set her leg down on the ground and leaned back on the log.

"It's broken. I don't really want to try to set it if we can get out of here any time soon. I think it's best to clean up the wounds and splint the break as it is. We need to keep it from moving around until a doctor can look at it. We'll keep your weight off of it and keep going as long as you're able." He raised a questioning eyebrow, looking for her agreement.

She simply nodded, clenching and unclenching her fists.

"I'll get you some of that pain medication you gave me. Once that takes effect, I'll fix this up and we'll move on."

AJ lay back in a semi-daze. Dan cleaned her wounds, pouring antiseptic from their small first aid kit onto the rusty punctures as AJ hissed. He secured her lower leg against a wooden splint, wrapping cloth above and below the break in her ankle. Every time she cried out in pain, a shiver raced through his body, and he felt as though he'd been hit. He was finishing when they heard the sound of a plane overhead. Looking up into clear blue sky, they saw an old single engine amphibious plane cruise over slowly, dropping in altitude. The sound got quieter, but didn't fade completely. Instead, it changed as the plane landed somewhere ahead.

"They're coming for us. You said they'd be back."

"Don't get too excited. Whoever it is, is still quite a distance away. Sounds carry a long way up here. Besides, it might not be a search plane at all, just a coincidence. We'd better get moving toward the sound just in case!"

"Right." He pulled her up, steadying her when she swayed.

"Can you make it, Aurora, or should I go find the plane and come back?"

A weak smile crossed her lips. "The way you navigate in the woods? Nothing doin'. We stick together. Come on, help me."

He looped her arm over his shoulders on his good side coupling her bad leg with his strong one. Together they hobbled in the direction of the engine sounds they had heard. With Stone gone, they only had to worry about making it to a search and rescue team.

***

The old plane taxied toward the bare spot of shore Jorgensen had seen the day before. The battered and rickety relic had replaced his sleek white and gold company plane. God alone knew if it could stay in the air. It had been the only plane his friend had at Dog Lake. He ran the nose up on shore, then climbed out to tie the craft to a tree. When he finished, he climbed on the pontoon and reached into the small cabin. He pulled out a .30-30, also borrowed from the man at Dog Lake. The fool believed him when he said he wanted to go on an unscheduled hunting trip. He snickered. *Well, I guess it is a hunting trip of sorts. I can't wait to see that little bitch's face just before I shoot her.*

He slammed the door of the plane and jumped to the shore. Jorgensen took a compass reading and walked into the woods, headed due north from the river.

"Let's take a break." Dan eased her down onto a log as she started to protest. He cut her off. "Be sensible. We have to take it easy just like you did on me, or we won't get to the river at all."

AJ agreed reluctantly and allowed him to settle her on the downed tree for a brief rest. Eager to keep moving, they both realized they would have to be careful not to push their luck any further, or AJ wouldn't be able to continue for long. All they could do was move at a cautious pace and hope that whoever had landed on the river was part of the search team that was looking for them, not just someone taking a break who would fly off and leave them behind before they could get his attention.

Checking the wraps on her leg, he loosened them to allow for the increased swelling taking place. He didn't want the circulation to her foot being cut off. When he finished, he smoothed his fingertips across her damp forehead trying to remove the creases pain had etched between her eyes. A frown wrinkled his own forehead as he noted the tight lines around her mouth. He lifted her wrist and felt for her pulse. It was shallow and rapid, much too rapid. She was still in shock.

He had to get her out of the forest and to a hospital soon. Terror clamped its tentacled fingers around his heart. How did his happiness get so dependent on her presence in only a few short days? What would he do if they weren't found soon, and she slipped away from him? He wouldn't, couldn't let that happen.

"Ready?" he asked quietly.

She nodded. A cry slipped from her as he helped her up. She balanced on her good foot as he looped her arm over his shoulders and slipped his arm around her waist, taking the weight of her body on his own.

The sound of another plane made them hesitate and look skyward again. Like the first plane, the sound didn't fade away but changed as it landed also.

A broad grin split Dan's face as he looked down at her. A crooked smile sat on her lips.

"It's getting as busy as Grand Central. They've honed in on us. Just a short while, and we'll get out of here," he said.

Roy had Ben taxi their plane up to Jorgensen's. Ben tied the planes together, then the others climbed out to join him on land. Charlie put his hand over the engine cover on the ancient plane.

"Still warm. He hasn't been gone long."

A Canadian police detective had joined them and carried a warrant for Jorgensen's arrest. "Don't worry. We'll catch him and find your family." He checked his weapon, compass, and map.

Charlie and Geoffrey paced. Roy sat on a log, his hands clasped together, fingers twined together in knots. Silently he rocked just as he had rocked AJ for hours in her infancy. His stomach was flipping like it had the only time in his life he had gotten the nerve to try skydiving. His baby was out there somewhere. If she was still alive, Jorgensen was after her.

"Can't you guys hurry up?" Roy snapped.

Geoffrey gave him a thumbs up, and he and the policeman started out followed by Ben and Marjorie. Geoffrey impatiently swung back around.

"Where do you think you're going?"

Marjorie pulled herself up to her full petite height, a determined look reflected in her features. "If you think I'm going to sit here while Dan is out there in trouble, you are further off your trolley than I thought."

"You are not going!" Geoffrey emphasized each word. "Charlie, see that she stays with you two," he ordered.

Charlie turned a nervous look on his old friend and shrugged. Roy gave an imperceptible shake of his head as he watched the struggle for control going on between Dan's parents.

Marjorie held up her hand, pointing a finger at Charlie's chest. "You stay away from me. I see this two ways, Geoffrey. We can stand here, waste precious time, and then go, or we can just go. I'm going either way. It's up to you how much time we lose."

A look of admiration skipped across Geoffrey's face before it was quickly disguised by one of annoyance. "If you slow us down, we'll leave you behind."

"I've never slowed you down, Geoffrey, nor have you ever been able to leave me behind." She tilted her head regally as though giving him permission to set off through the forest.

Roy thought of Jorgensen and what he might do to AJ before his friends reached her. "Quit foolin' around and get goin'! You two can have a power struggle later."

He watched Geoffrey hide a smile as he turned and led the way between the trees.

Roy's stomach did another back flip into a seemingly bottomless pit as he helplessly watched the others move into the brush around the lake and disappear in the forest. Never had he felt so powerless, nor had he cursed his disability more, than at this moment.

Charlie stood silently by his side, his hand resting reassuringly on Roy's shoulder.

Roy knew his old friend wanted to offer some consolation, but how could he? There is no consolation when you think you may have lost a child. All they could do was wait as the others started after Jorgensen in the hope of catching him and finding AJ and Dan. All Roy could do was trust that Geoffrey and the others would bring his daughter back to him alive.

CHAPTER FOURTEEN

Jorgensen wound between the trees, skirting underbrush. Sweat ran down his body, plastering his light blue Oxford shirt to his chest. He refused to stoop to flannel shirts like a common lumberjack. His khaki pants were stuffed into the tops of hiking boots.

He stopped to listen for any sound that would indicate MacKenzie and Satterfield were close by. He strained to hear the sound of their voices carrying through the forest or of coveys of quail or other animals flushed out by their movements. Anything to tell him his quarry was near.

A short time later, clutching the rifle with twitching fingers, he stopped again and waited, listening as he held his breath so he could hear every sound, every twig that snapped, every pine cone that dropped from the canopy of trees. The forest remained silent, giving up nothing.

***

AJ and Dan broke through a dense patch of underbrush. They faced a steep bluff covered with scattered boulders, pine and cedar trees—and slippery pine needles.

"Dan?"

He stopped and turned toward her, an unspoken question hanging between them. One look at her ashen face told him all he needed to know.

"I need a break." Before she finished the sentence he had swung her into his arms and limped over to a large granite boulder. Her head dropped onto his broad shoulder as her arms looped his neck and held on. His heart thumped against her breast. He eased her down onto a small boulder and turned her so he could place her broken ankle on the rock next to it.

"Let me loosen up the wraps and have a look at that." Her jaw clamped tight but she nodded and leaned back on her hands so he could get at the splint. Pulling aside her jeans, Dan frowned at the bluish tint of her skin. He unfastened the clip holding the wraps in place and gently eased the fit around the swelling tissue.

The amount of discoloration and swelling was frightening. More damage had been done than he thought. The teeth marks from the rusted trap were red and angry. It scared him to think that if she didn't get medical help soon, infection would set in and complicate the healing of her break.

"When'd you have a tetanus shot?"

"I don't know. When I went to college, I guess. It's been a while."

"When we get you to a doctor, he'll have to give you one. There are bits of rust and dirt still in these wounds."

Finished with his assessment Dan refastened the wraps and sat next to her to pull her gently back against his chest to rest.

Sweeping her hair over her shoulder, he tenderly kissed her neck beneath her collar. He marveled at the scent of her. How she could be so fresh and enticing in these circumstances? The natural scent that clung to her was far more seductive than women in the city paid hundreds for. AJ assaulted his senses with her simplicity.

Her clothes were ragged and dirty, her skin was scratched and abused, and she had pine needles and twigs caught in her hair. *She's beautiful, so beautiful.*

He removed the bits from the black mass of hair. The sunlight drifted between the towering trees, fracturing the light, highlighting the colors of the northern lights reflected her hair. He was reminded how beautiful she was. Not to mention intelligent, strong, and resourceful. You couldn't ask for a better friend or mate. He didn't want to be without her, ever.

He wanted her to accept how he felt. She seemed to be so cautious, afraid of a commitment. He opened his mouth to tell her he loved her, stopped and snapped it shut as a sound carried through the trees.

"Did you hear anything?"

She shook her head and shrugged. She wasn't alert to what was happening around her. That terrified him.

"What was it?" she asked.

"I don't know. I thought I heard something crashing through the brush farther up the hill. Maybe it's a search party. I'll go and check."

His comment broke through her haze. AJ reached out and grabbed his sleeve. "Dan, a search party would be yelling for us."

"I'm going to check it out," he whispered, seeing the concern on AJ's face. "I won't take any chances." He pulled Stone's rifle from the ties that secured it his backpack. "Don't move on that leg without me. You stay put," he ordered quietly.

As he turned away, she caught his arm again. "Be careful, Dan. I love you. Don't do anything stupid."

Something tugged at his heart. Something he'd never felt before. "I love you, too. I'll be back."

He smiled and gave her a brief kiss, then pulled away. "I'll be back, honey. You can count on it."

***

AJ listened to his movements as he made his way around the base of the bluff, and then started working his way toward the top. The sound of footsteps reached her from the opposite side of the bluff. She realized whoever it was would probably not see Dan. She intended to keep it that way.

Sliding off the boulder, she lowered herself to the ground behind it, crying out as she did. AJ scooted up as close as she could to the base of the rock trying to hide from whoever caused the approaching sounds. She wanted to see what or who it was before letting herself be seen.

Crunching footsteps slowed, then stopped. Whoever it was appeared to be waiting, listening, or scenting the air like a wolf. Pushed back against the granite boulder, she prayed that Dan was still looking on the wrong side of the hill. The footsteps started again. The crackling increased. She sank back trying to become one with the stone. Her ankle connected with a jutting piece of the boulder ripping a shriek form her lips. As the sound escaped, her mouth clamped shut cutting off any more noise. It was too late.

Jorgensen sprang around the boulder to her hiding place. A grotesque Halloween pumpkin grin split his face. Her gaze fell on the gun in his hands and froze. She had to get him away from Dan.

"Well, well. So you did make it through the crash. How about that? Too bad, though." His eyes narrowed. "All that walking to make it out was a waste. You'll never see home again."

AJ took a chance on a bluff. "Jorgensen, boy am I glad to see you. Are you part of the search team? Where's everybody else? Who was in the second plane that landed with you?"

She watched as his face blanched, then the smile faded from his face.

"I'm not stupid. I..."

"Of course you're not stupid. I never said you were, only that we had some minor disagreements over business. Get me out of this mess, and I'd be very grateful. You said yourself the others would listen to me." She paused. "I can help you."

"You don't expect me to believe that you don't know how this happened, do you?" He glared at her.

Her pulse rolled like summer thunder as she started to answer, but he went on before she could.

"Where's that client of yours? Satterfield isn't it?"

AJ dropped her chin to her chest. "Was." A tear rolled down her cheek. A tear from the renewed pain in her leg, but he didn't have to know that. "He died in the crash. I killed him when I lost control of the plane. All my fault." She sniffled and pulled a bandanna from her pocket. As she held it to her face, the scent of Dan filled her nostrils. *I have to get this lunatic away from here.*

"Please, can't we head back. I...I need a doctor. My ankle's broken."

"We'll head out all right, but you won't need a doctor when I get through with you." He reached down and yanked her to her feet as she groaned. Pain shot through her causing her head to spin. She swayed, focused on Dan's image, anything to stay upright. She balanced on her good foot and silently prayed for the pain and dizziness to pass.

"Why are you doing this, Jorgensen? Murder's a much worse charge than fraud."

She looked at him and shrank away from the evil and madness reflected in his eyes. They were glacial.

"You ruined it all. Now I have to get rid of you and that client of yours, or it will all be for nothing."

"I told you he died," she said frantically. "He..."

Jorgensen grabbed her arm and started dragging her up the slope behind them. "I told you I'm not stupid. Everybody always said I was stupid. My parents, teachers, everybody. But I'll show you and all of them." The slight control on his emotions seemed to evaporate as something in his mind snapped. "Come on. We're going for a walk."

Drenched with sweat, her stomach rolled with waves of nausea. The dizziness returned, and she slumped toward the ground. Jorgensen jerked her to her feet tearing a scream of pain from her.

The image of Dan running to her rescue and being shot down made the scream freeze in her throat. Wait and see what he's up to, she thought. Two can play any game but solitaire.

"I can't walk, Jorgensen. If you want to get anywhere fast, you're going to have to help me."

"We aren't going far. I'll dump you then find Satterfield."

He dragged her along beside him as she half-hopped and half crawled, dragging her bad leg behind her. She was leaving a trail a blind man could follow, but there wasn't anything she could do about that.

Not convinced Dan was a match for the madman, AJ prayed he would stay away. She hoped that she and Jorgensen would be away from here before Dan returned and followed them. Her hopes died a sudden death.

"Jorgensen!" Dan yelled.

The small man halted and swung around in one motion when he heard his name.

"Run, Dan!"

"Shut up," Jorgensen growled and shook her. He dragged her in front of his body as a shield.

Her head spun from the pain shooting up her calf. Her knees buckled and she sagged against Jorgensen. When she tried to slide to the ground, Jorgensen's arm slipped around her chest under her breasts, forcing her to stay on her feet.

"Stay back, Satterfield. I'll kill her if you don't. You may as well come out."

AJ looked around frantically, but she couldn't see where Dan was hidden.

"Dan...?"

Jorgensen clamped his arm across her throat making anything but slight gasping murmurs impossible.

"Jorgensen, let her go. We don't care about you or your deals. Drop her and take off."

"I can't do that and you know it," Jorgensen answered. "You might as well come out. I'll find you anyway."

Dan yelled from the cover of the trees. "The way I see it, you're going to kill her whether I come out or not. The little fool crashed our plane in the middle of nowhere, and we've been walking ever since. Why should I care what you do to her?"

Jorgensen dropped his arm from her throat to circle her ribs. He cupped one breast suggestively. She shrank from the disgusting touch of his hand as she heard the curse slip from Dan.

"I'd say you care a lot more than you want me to think. Now come out here, or I swear I'll kill her."

Jorgensen shifted his hold and dragged her up the slope with him.

Tears ran unchecked down her face. If Dan came out, Jorgensen would gun him down. "Please go back," she called. Dan ignored her. She saw flashes of color from his jacket as he moved through the underbrush to keep up with them.

Jorgensen and AJ reached the top of the bluff. Backing toward it, he continued to shout for Dan to come out.

"The way I see it, you're going to kill her no matter what I do, Jorgensen. I'll take my chances down here."

"You're only postponing the inevitable, Satterfield. I'll be done with her in a second, then I'm coming for you. Maybe I'll have some fun with this little bitch before I kill her. Would you like that, Satterfield? Would you like to watch?" He cackled and shrieked as a rivulet of saliva dribbled unheeded down his chin. He was beyond the edge of sanity.

Dan slowly stood up. AJ couldn't see his rifle. He called out once more. "Jorgensen! If you hurt her, I'll kill you with my bare hands. Let her go!"

Jorgensen turned to the cliff face and looked over. AJ clawed at his arm trying to hang on. They balanced on the edge of the escarpment. She saw Dan standing below them and knew that as soon as Jorgensen finished her, he would turn on the man she loved.

Fear and fury pumped adrenaline through her veins, spreading like burning oil on water. She swung her hip to the side and slammed her fist into Jorgensen's groin. The breath whooshed from his body as he doubled over. In the same split second, the sound of a .30-30 rang out through the forest.

Jorgensen jerked back and grabbed his shoulder. Then he was falling. Arms flailing, he clutched at AJ's arm. He dragged her over the side and into midair with him. The instant she lost her balance, she saw the panic on Dan's face as he raced for the top of the cliff. Then she toppled backwards over the edge.

"AJ!" Dan screamed. He ran, dragging air into his lungs and plunging around rocks and trees on his way up the hill. "Answer me," he pleaded as he ran.

At the top of the hill, he fell onto his stomach and looked over the side searching for AJ. The dust that enveloped her settled. She dangled from a bush almost six feet from the top. Her hands were wrapped around the tiny branches that clung to the cliff. She dug the tip of her boot into the dirt to get a toehold. Sheer terror and pain were mirrored on her face. At the bottom of the ravine, Jorgensen lay motionless, his body smashed against the rocks piled there.

Jorgensen was no longer a threat. The drop was.

"Hang on, honey. I'm here." He stretched down to her leaning as far over the side as he dared. "AJ grab my hand."

She shook her head and buried her eyes in her sleeve.

"Come on. You can do this. Give me your hand," he ordered.

AJ slowly shifted and looked up. Their eyes locked. She reached with one hand. The bush gave up part of its hold. She slipped further down, frantically digging in with the toe of her good foot. Grabbing wildly, she grasped the roots of the plant where they stuck out from the washed away slope. Madly she clutched at the twisted vines.

Dan's heart almost stopped, then his pulse raced like a runaway train. He forced the calm he didn't feel into his voice.

"Come on, honey. Trust me. Please, I can't reach you without help. Let go with one hand and stretch up here as far as you can."

She started to release her gripping fingers. The bush again gave a little. He watched her slip farther away. Her knuckles were white from her death grip.

"I can't, Dan. I'll fall."

"Trust me, Aurora. Please. I love you. I won't let you go. Aurora," he coaxed, "listen to me. Grab my hands."

The clinging roots gave up pulling from earth one by one. Dan watched her slipping away. Fear gripped his throat, constricting his air and voice. As the last twigs gave way, terror released its hold, allowing him to function.

"Grab me—now!" he commanded.

When he reached for her this time, she grabbed his arm with one hand.

The movement caused the bush to give up its slight hold on the cliff face. He saw the terror in her eyes as she fell backward away from the dirt wall, screamed and clawed the dirt with her hands.

Dan dove part way over the side grabbing her wrists in his hands as he dug in with his feet to keep from being jerked over by her weight. The muscles in his forearms tightened and bunched. He stopped her fall and held her still. His breathing was ragged and came in short gasps.

Sweat rolled freely down his face as he concentrated on keeping them both from free falling to the bottom. Slowly he inched backward from the brink of disaster as he pulled her toward him. Moments later he rolled back from the side, dragging her to safety.

For long seconds they lay head to head gasping in air. When he could move, Dan scooted around to lie beside her. He eased his body up to hers and gently lifted her into his arms. Tremors rumbled through his body, wave after wave. He'd almost lost the most important thing in the world.

When the shaking subsided, Dan rose on his elbow and looked at her. "I thought..." His voice broke. He cleared his throat and tried again. "I thought you were gone. Are you all right?"

A tear slipped down her dirty cheek leaving a track in its wake. Another and another quickly followed it. Dan sat up and lifted her so he could slide under her body, balancing her on his thighs. He rocked her as he cradled her head against his shoulder, soothing her like a lost child. She trembled and clung to his body, sobbing quietly and soaking the front of his jacket.

At last, she pulled back and raised her eyes to his. "I was so afraid. I thought he was going to kill you."

"Me? It was you he was trying to throw over the cliff." He smiled at her gently, brushing his lips across her forehead, then trailing them down her cheeks. He tasted the salty tears mixed with the dust on her face and pulled a handkerchief from his pocket to gently wipe it all from her pale skin.

He stuffed the dirty cloth back in his pocket and gathered her once more to his chest. AJ relaxed against him while he spoke soft words against her hair. He spoke of home, of love, of future plans. The words themselves didn't appear to register in her pain-numbed mind, only the reassurance they were meant to convey.

Dan's quiet voice worked its magic, and he saw her relax. It lasted only a moment, then she stiffened and pulled away.

"Did you hear that?" she asked.

"No." He captured her lips in a tender kiss as she tried to protest. For a moment she gave herself to him. The sound came again, closer this time.

She pushed against Dan's shoulders, laughing and struggling to free herself. "Listen!"

Regretfully, he raised his head, trying to hear what had drawn her attention. Finally, he heard it, too. A shout echoed through the woods below them.

"AJ, Dan!" The sound bounced from tree to tree and was repeated several times.

"Stay here." Dan gently laid her against a boulder then jumped to his feet and moved back to balance on the edge of the cliff. He cupped his hands around his mouth and shouted when he saw several people break into the clearing at he base of the cliff.

"We're up here. On the top of the hill." He heard an answering shout.

Expecting strangers, members of a search and rescue team, Dan was shocked when he recognized his mother and father.

"Dad! We're up here."

"Are you both all right?" Geoffrey shouted.

"Sort of. I'll need help getting AJ down. She's got a broken ankle. We'll need to carry her."

"Right. We'll be right up."

Dan watched as his father gave orders. Everybody was moving at once.

"Ben, go back and let Roy know everything's all right," his father said. "Get on the radio and call off the search and rescue, but let them know we need a medical team up here."

From where he bent over Jorgensen's body, the detective called out, "Have them send a police team and medical examiner, too. I'm going to need some help here."

The group split up and Marjorie waved up at Dan, tears running down her cheeks. His father picked her up and swung her around before setting her on the ground and sweeping her into a long kiss. A kiss that said far more than "We found our son."

Dan laughed as he watched her push Geoffrey away. He could tell she wasn't as offended as she wanted his father to think.

When they broke apart, Dan pointed to the far side of the bluff and a deer trail there. "Come up that way." He dropped down beside AJ, a contented smile lighting his face.

"They've found us, Aurora. We'll get you out and to a hospital soon now. Can you handle the pain just a while longer?"

"Now that we know it'll be over soon, I can."

To take her mind off the wait, Dan changed the subject. "By the way, do you remember that matchmaking plan you cooked up to get my parents together?"

She nodded.

A Cheshire cat grin split his face. "I don't think we're going to need it. My folks came looking for us together, and from what I just saw, they have a few embers left alive that seem to be rekindling as well as one of your campfires."

She smiled warmly as her eyelids fluttered closed. Softly, Dan ran his fingers over her face. He dropped a light kiss on her forehead. Dan drew her into his arms as he leaned back on the boulder. She sighed with pleasure.

The vision of AJ falling intruded on the peaceful moment. He shuddered and pulled her closer to his chest.

"Aurora," he murmured, "I thought I'd lost you. Seeing you fall backwards over that edge... I don't know what I'd do without you." A shuddering breath slipped from his lips. "The moment you dropped out of sight over the cliff was the worst experience I've ever had." He shivered as the unbidden picture flashed through his mind's eye.

"It wasn't exactly my favorite thing either, you know. If I was into free falling I'd be jumping out of planes, not flying them." They snuggled together, waiting for help.

Geoffrey and Marjorie soon joined them. His parents stood for a moment, then his mother was racing toward him, tears on her cheeks. Dan laid AJ aside then jumped up to hug his mother, reaching behind her to shake hands with his father. His father held tightly to Dan's strong hand, then with a weak smile and a shrug, he pulled his grown son into his arms and hugged him.

After an awkward silence, everyone began talking at once. Geoffrey and Dan were trying to ask and answer questions, then the policeman joined them and started firing questions at Dan.

"All right!" his mother snapped.

The men stopped chattering and turned to her.

"Let's get this young woman out of here. She's not getting any better lying in the middle of a forest." Marjorie placed her fists on her hips. "We'll have plenty of time later to play twenty questions. Two of you cradle her between you and let's go."

A smile curved Dan's lips as he watched his mother ramrod the grown men. He wasn't about to disagree with her.

"Right, then. Let's go," he said.

They picked her up and headed toward the plane that waited on the Fort Albany River. A short time later they broke through the trees onto the shoreline.

AJ spotted her father and Charlie. "Dad!" she shrieked.

Dan lowered her onto the log beside her father. She threw her arms around his neck laughing and crying as he clutched her to his chest, his hands tangled in her long hair. Charlie stood nearby, wiping a suspicious drop from his eye as he watched the reunion for a moment before he, too, moved over and gave her a bear hug. Dan watched the warm reunion wishing he and his father had such a special bond.

The questions began again, but before Dan and AJ could tell

their story, the sound of the Medivac plane coming in for a landing cut them off. A police plane followed, and suddenly things were out of their control as they were shuttled back to Thunder Bay.

Hours later Dan knocked softly on the door of AJ's hospital room. When she didn't answer, he stuck his head around the door as he eased it open and slipped into the room. She slept, her face as white as the sheets that covered her. Her lower leg was in a cast; her cuts and scratches cared for.

AJ only had to rest and get well, he told himself. Why did he feel like this, then? Like he'd been kicked in the stomach by her blasted moose. His hands shook slightly as he laid the flowers he carried on the tray table. His knees gave out, and he sank down on the bed beside her. Dan lowered his forehead onto his folded hands, and for the first time, sent up a silent prayer of thanks.

AJ's eyes fluttered open. The lights created a swirling array of color. Her head felt like it could float away from her body. She touched Dan's hair and he raised sparkling eyes to look at her. Confused, she fought to focus on his face.

Deep grooves furrowed his brow. She would swear his eyes were moist. Slowly she raised her hand to lay her palm against his cheek. Turning his head, he kissed the soft flesh before grasping her hand in both of his and pulling it close to his chest. She could feel the strong beat of his heart where he held it over his breast.

"How you doin', kid?" His voice was gruff and soaked in emotion.

"Better now that you're here," she whispered. "Where is everybody?"

"They'll be back. Your dad and Charlie are getting cleaned up, and they'll be over soon. The doctors wanted you to rest for a bit before your visitors started coming by."

"What are you doing here, then?" She smiled, a slight bit of color coming back into her cheeks as she saw the flash of need that sparked in his eyes.

He reached over and gently slipped his fingertips down her jaw and under her chin, then over her throat and onto her shoulder as if he wanted to learn the feel of her all over again.

The touch of his fingers brought fire to her skin. Her lips parted as she slipped the tip of her tongue across her dry lips. The pad of his thumb rubbed over her lips and he felt the moisture her tongue had left there. When his lips met hers in a slow reverent kiss, AJ slipped her hands behind his neck pulling him down, drinking her fill from his mouth. The kiss deepened and the exhilaration of doing a successful outside loop hit her. Her spirits lifted as she spiraled higher and higher.

Dan pulled her arms from his neck with obvious reluctance, fighting visibly to get a grip on his self-control.

Enjoying the moment, AJ smiled and slipped her hand up his thigh. He grabbed her hands and drew them together at his chest to stop their wandering as he groaned and lowered his chin onto her hands.

"You, young lady, are incorrigible. You are in here to rest and recuperate. I don't think that includes what you have in mind."

She chuckled as she laid her head back on her pillow. "All right. I guess I can wait, if I have to." A soft sigh slipped from her lips. "Looks like our vacation is over."

His smile faded and his shoulders stiffened. "This one maybe, but there'll be others. I won't leave you and this beautiful country to go back to a solitary life in the city." He drew in a deep breath. "Tell me you want me to stay, Aurora. Tell me you can't live without me just as I can't be without you." He kissed her fingertips.

"I want to be your partner. In business, in life. We're going to fly and camp and fish and teach our children to love the outdoors as much as we do." He rattled on not giving her a chance to accept or refuse his plans.

AJ laughed as her heart began to soar. He needed her. He wanted her, and he wanted to have children with her. "Haven't you forgotten something?"

He looked at her obviously puzzled.

"Don't you think we should get married before we start having children?"

Dan nodded. "I have it all worked out. While you recover, I'll go back to Chicago and wrap up business. I already talked to my father, and he understands why I want to leave the company. As soon as you're well, we'll get married."

"That sounds like an order, not a proposal."

"It is an order," he growled, then added quietly, "if you'll let me marry you. You'd better or we'll just have to live in sin and have our children out of wedlock, because I'm never going to let you go."

"You're a devil, Dan Satterfield."

A sinful smile curved his lips as he lowered his mouth to hers. Her lips opened to meet his tongue as he touched and tempted her mouth into an immediate searing response.

He spoke in between the nips he was taking on her lips. "There are all sorts of things I want to teach you, and I want you to teach me to dance in the air. Have any complaints about that, Sky Dancer?"

AJ gazed at Dan with eyes that sparkled with unshed tears and shook her head. "No. You teach me to love like the devil, and I'll teach you to dance with the angels."

About the Author

Kathleen Wells' first love is writing romance fiction where the main theme is that only unconditional love is true love and that unconditional love conquers all. She loves getting readers involved in the lives of real characters they care about, in wonderful settings all wrapped in a believable and entertaining plot. Her goal is to encourage readers to settle for nothing less than the unconditional love they deserve.

Kathleen lives in southeastern Arizona with her family, horses and dog. She loves to hear from readers who may contact her at kathleenwells@mindspring.com, or Please visit her at http://www.kathleenwells.com